# SPARE US YET

## AND OTHER STORIES

# SPARE US YET

## AND OTHER STORIES

## LUCAS SMITH

Wiseblood Books

To Mum/Mom and Dad

# CONTENTS

# PRELUDE: UNIT 1002

The rod of gold has faded out again. It is all I know of night and day in unit 1002, hovering as I have since Anno Christi one thousand eight hundred and fifty-eight, when God sent and Father Kilcunda called me down with fanfare to Christ's altar in front of a capacity crowd in the Lady Chapel of Saint Chad's, Chisholmwell. The view was great in those early years, majestic, all the apostles gleaming in their windows, and the stream of penitents and daily communicants.

For well over a century, I have patrolled this altar. Several times I had to scare away some dodgy characters by banging on the window (sorry, St. Bartholomew!). One couple had even undressed in preparation for a desecration that I could not allow. I started the organ playing Bach's toccata, and I don't know what the vicar thought of the red pumps he found the next morning. Other angels look askance at interaction with humans, but *in extremis* it is allowed. A full incident report is on file with Archangel Michael. Once I saved the tabernacle from falling in an earthquake.

Despite remaining here for all those years, never venturing beyond the nave and sanctuary, I have my ways of knowing the ways of men. Snippets of chat after Mass. The many vicars' few expressions. But then Saint Chad's, Chisholmwell fell into decrepitude. The young, it seemed, no longer cared for themselves or Creation or their Lord. And the little children I knew grew up and went above and the place was decommissioned, deconsecrated by the Archbishop. The parish merged with Saint Cuthbert's down the road.

But he forgot to say the prayers of deconsecration of the altar that would have loosed me, and I'm a stickler for the rules. That's how God made me. My altar was sent to unit 1002. Mrs. Fairbanks covered up our Lord's resting place with boxes full of books. The place where once a day, or sometimes twice, since 1858, the Lord of All appears on earth. *Forgive her, Lord. Amen.* They placed the two angel candlesticks, which by the way look nothing like me, on the floor, surrounded by the robes and cassocks and paraphernalia that Saint Cuthbert's had no use for. In the dusk, cluttered with smells of stale elastic and moths, the presence that makes my presence presses in, warmly, and pressurises unit 1002 with His charge and the smallest speck of powder and stalest plastic lives, and rises upward through soiled cassocks to me, the storage complex, Saint Chad's decommissioned steeple-top, and the still-veiled stars He suffuses.

Michael comes to visit once a decade. He says they're working on the problem but can't promise anything at the moment. Men and their ways cause delay. Tricky business. I could go rogue and leave, but the work is necessary even here. The demons always prowl, infesting unit 1002, threatening thousands upon thousands of neglectful souls, jealous of the good, wary of my flaming sword. And what does an Angel have but his word?

And then one golden-rod-lit day, I hear voices outside unit 1002. An auction. Unit 1002 sells for $275. Then the voices move on. The next day the door rolls up and the light streams in like a flash of beatific vision. They pile the boxes of books away, and I rejoice to see that sacred spot freed once more. They load the altar onto the bed of a truck and me with it. Some demons follow half-heartedly along the road, but they trail away as they despise the light. To think I have not been outside for more than fifty years! The truck enters a yard where heaps of wood are piled up, broken chairs and tables, shattered crates. It is not so bad, and the men who work here look in need of Our Lord.

Then the crack and the buzz, like what some crazed demons do with their gnashing of teeth. It's a machine at the end of the yard where the wood is fed in and ground up. I contemplate giving the men torn ligaments or pulled fingers to stop this madness, this desecration, but while I could, I cannot. A wrong is wrong; I would become a demon. The Lord will tolerate no tormenting for His sake. O Father Kilcunda, this is the end of the assignment God, through you, gave me. I fix my gaze on that lovely haunting place, then into the pile of particles, into the sparkling blades, and out and up into the heavenly realms again. Bliss. But have I failed? *Lord, forgive them. Amen.*

# LIONS OVER THE BRIDGE

Jesus is my fuck-you money. That's what I wanted to say to Clay. I know he loves me, being my older brother, but he's not ride or die. I got my integrity, I got a tent under cover near the State Library, I got Prince and I got Jesus, motherfucker. I shouldn't use those words: sorry, Lord. The sun is going down, but I'm sundowner stock. Know how to do just enough. Dropped the keys and two hundred and fifty dollars for the cleaning off at the estate agent's office, and I'm on the footpath in Newtown flexing like a weightlifter gearing up for the gold medal lift, opening my mouth to the driving rain and embracing the wind. Is this all you got, God? I like to bantz Him sometimes, tease him a bit, let Him know I can take more.

"Here's five hundred. That's all I can spare," Clay said. "You're putting your life in danger. Again. You need fuck-you money to have your attitude. Why don't you just stay with us for a while?"

But I didn't want to burden him like that. I thought of St. Isaac the Syrian: be like the bees and go where the good stuff is, not like the flies who go anywhere. In fact, I was looking forward to some time on the streets. Reminded me of my young days, camping out, even hitch-hiking a bit outside the city. Man, that dates me. I also reckon Sydney is one of the best places to be homeless. Beaut climate, stunning views, lots of money around. Just a spell on the lam from the crazies. Can't take anything away from someone who's got fuck-all. Sorry, Mate.

Clay never took Jesus into his heart. He's an upright man but obsessed with his house and always talking about getting another one, always on the real-estate websites. Reckons he'll put his feet up when he's got a few properties rented out, but he won't. He'll always be anxious because he's got no one to be grateful to. He never went down like I did into the grog and worse. Never went up to God like I did, or like I'm trying to. Just stayed straight and on the ground but I have to love him because You do.

I'd already paid the rent for March, but I couldn't be arsed. I dragged my shit out onto the curb: the futon, my couch, the paintings Lisa had left me (Godspeed), my table and chairs. Most people would assume, seeing all that stuff out front, that the tenant had just been booted. I wished I could place a sign on my pile of furniture saying HOMELESS DUE TO JAB, but I didn't. I'll just be doing a Bradbury for the time being.

I knew it was the drop-dead day from all the emails, but they weren't addressed to me personally, so I pretended I never got them. I went in to work as usual and I was up the scaffold all morning with Cameron fiddling with a tricky joist and I heard the foreman calling up to us. Calling my name.

"You're in strife now, mate," Cameron said. "Cheeky bugger."

"Best wishes, mate, if I don't see you again."

No sooner do my boots hit the mud and he says, "I need to see your vaccination certificate," while backing away like I'm a dangerous dog.

He's a young guy with a smooth face, a clipboard. He wears a green fleecy vest.

"I don't have one."

"Then you have to leave now."

"Can I just help Cameron finish?"

"No. You have to leave now."

After I dropped my keys back at the estate agent, I set out for the city with my swag, Prince's bed, bowl and lead, my Bible, my Desert Fathers, the new Les Murray I stole from GleeBooks, my notepad, pen, and glass water bottle. I avoid plastic if I can. Do not worry about what you will eat, what you will wear. Jesus and Diogenes, with varied emphasis day by day, that's me. Nah, Jesus is always number one, Lord of all.

I set up my tent at the Palace at the top of Martin Place. The Palace is what they call the scaffolding that covers all our tents. Whatever this great big sandstone building is, it's been being built or upgraded for ages, and it's like the scaff is a permanent feature now. It was already there when I spent a night or two after Lisa booted me out for letting our dealer keep his stash at our place, must have been more than ten years ago now. My spot is right below the big lions carved into the façade, the ones that look like the ones on the English cricket coat of arms. The rows of tents are almost as far as the eye can see down to the bottom of Martin Place, more than I remember. This is where the man in the poem wept. The things you hear at night. People calling out for their mothers or lovers. And then there's the ones who don't move for two days and you wonder if you should stop one of the cops and have them check if they're dead. But they're usually not dead. The smell around the Palace is not so bad the colder it gets. I don't think I cry out for anyone. At least no one has said anything to me.

It's a total fucking gas, as they say, stepping out into the unknown. When you're on the streets most people either ignore you, which is fine, or they're extra nice. Especially clergymen. Especially this young priest. He squatted down outside the tent and listened to my whole story, even about Lisa. Said it was a tough decision to make and everyone has to do what they feel is right in the sight of the Lord. He didn't want it either but took it, he said, to stay close to his parishioners and people like me. A sacrifice like the Lord. I said I'm not getting Bill Gates's juice in my arm, sorry to be vulgar. Even if it was liquid gold, I wouldn't get it.

I slipped a fifty into the priest's leather satchel when he wasn't watching. Old Brice was bailing him up with his usual litany: how he used to be a top winger right before league went commercial, how he was an engineer in Texas, how he defended himself and won in the Supreme Court. Prince growls at him because he knows he's lying.

Trying to interject when Brice gets going with his furphies is something only the Lord has patience for, but I get in by asking the priest about himself.

"Not to be blunt, Father, but no sex? No family?"

"We all sacrifice for God."

True, Father.

I'm writing a book to record everything happening to us. Really how pathetic it all is. No 3 a.m. door-knocks, no camps, no show trials, or disappearances. Rubber bullet cops. Daniel and the housecats. I used to walk past the police with no mask on all the time. None of them ever said anything. I ripped the caution tape off the plastic grasshopper and bumblebee at the playground, liberating the swings, taking down the signs. In my mind it was for Lisa, not that it could do her any good.

The tyranny came from thinking you were alone. The tyranny was in the incoherence, the arbitrariness, the pig-headedness of the regulations, the way they twisted the virtues against you. It came in the form of middle-aged women who yelled over their shoulder at you in the street: "Wear a mask!" It came in the way people walked into oncoming traffic to avoid your naked face. I expected the powers that be to want to do something like this. What I didn't expect was for so many to go along with it. Forgive them, Lord, for they know not what they do.

I ask the young priest who made him take it. "The Arch. The Archbishop."

"That guy will have to answer to God just like the rest of us."

"Of course."

Lisa didn't want it either.

When you wake up without knowing how the day will unfold you feel like a hunter. It's the same exhilaration I remember as a boy on my grandparents' bush property. Three hundred acres of overgrown bushland to get lost in. Snakes, foxes, kangaroos. Wombat holes to crawl down. No one to tell you no, or to drop what you're doing and do summat else. I made a trout farm by myself there. I dammed up the creek with rocks and sticks and brush. No trout, of course. My grandparents came looking for me when they saw the lake rising up towards the house. They thought I was drowned. I was heaving rocks onto the dam, tossing them as high into the air as I could for joy, and listening to their splits and knocks.

Clay and I would go bow-hunting for deer, and when we couldn't find any, which was most of the time, we took pot shots at rabbits. I can't remember ever hitting any, but Clay says he has a memory of a rabbit pinned to the ground with an arrow through its back leg, spinning around with a whine like a wheezing curlew.

On the streets it's the dumb ones I feel for the most. The ones who never had a chance. The ones who couldn't be trusted to hold the right end of a knife. They're constantly confused, they believe everything and nothing. This woman who's about forty but looks eighty says the State Trustees are screwing her around, denying her withdrawals from her account, the bastards. I believe it too. She asks me for money to tide her over and I give it to her. A hundred bucks is nothing.

She draws in chalk on the flagstones all around her outside Macca's and one Saturday night, with the place chockers with people, a scooter delivery girl drove over her work. She was a Chinese girl and the lady started beating her and the scooter with her walking stick. I told her to leave the girl alone and she said that's easy for you to say being so big. You lose your pity out here pretty fast if you don't cultivate an open heart.

I never beg and I never drink. I take what's offered me and ask if I need to. Sometimes "it's flat food round the midriff and long food up the sleeve." Twiggy sticks and mountain bread, but only from the big guys. If I have too much or if I don't like where something's come from, like with Clay, I pass it on. For lunch there's the Salvo's on Wednesday and Saturday, the Anglo-Catholics on Thursday, and the Romans on Tuesday and Friday. The Anglo-Catholics have the best food: roast beef, chicken thighs, real coffee. You can usually take enough for Thursday dinner too. The Salvos always have Lamingtons, which give me the heebie-jeebies. I never eat Lamingtons. My father treated someone who'd eaten a Lamington made from mattress foam. It was a prank gone wrong. They covered this block of foam with coconut and chocolate. Actually, Dad didn't treat him because he was dead at the scene.

I try to help out anyone at the Palace with my skills. Brice asked me to put together a little bed frame from some bits of wood he scrounged up. Just something to keep his mattress off the stones. It's worn through where his hips and shoulders rest.

The truth is I could have gone on the dole, eked out an existence, but now I'm free. I reckon they'll make you get it for the dole too, soon enough. Can't be arsed dealing with them anyway. I think it's different for a woman, but a man should be prepared to lose everything on a flip of the card. Our father was a flying doctor out in the western deserts. He had a colleague who wanted to stay back at the pub drinking, so my dad took his place on a flight back to Carnarvon. The next day his originally scheduled plane never came in. His friend, a nurse, a patient, and the pilot all "perished"—as they say. My father was meant to be on that plane, and that's what I mean. Life is a coin flip. But as long as you're here, God's got something for you to do, or at least to learn.

I saw that young priest at Mass on Sunday. I wanted to give them the rest of my brother's cash, but the verger took one look at me and moved on to the next pew without proffering the plate. Yes, the hygiene is an issue. I put on deodorant when I can't get to a shower.

By the time I get around to writing again it's Thursday and I can see the young priest with an older priest dressed in bright purple holding big sacks at the bottom of the Palace, calling in on the tents, giving out something from the sack to each vagrant. I can't make out what it is from this distance. They're with a big group of men, and then I get it. The corporate sleepout: it's where they live our life for a night then talk about it on TV. That's what's in the sack, our goodie bags so we behave. I'm surprised they didn't use the fucking virus as an excuse to cancel it.

When they get to me I think he can tell I'm not like the others. Fuck, what am I thinking? Jesus keep me humble, I didn't mean that. I am not above anyone.

"This is Archbishop—" the young priest gives the name.

"With all due respect, Your Excellency, why'd you make all your priests take the jab?" I asked.

"It was a directive from the government."

"What about directives from God?"

"The individual conscience must be sovereign. I would have preferred that my priests choose to protect others without a command."

The young priest stares at the flagstones.

. . .

After Anglo-Catholic lunch, I walk across the bridge over to the rich suburbs, fingering my rosary the whole way. It's a glorious day. I wear my best clothes and leave my suitcase with Brice. I don't want to scare anyone. There's that beaut walk out to Cremorne Point. I used to come here with Lisa. By the end of it you almost don't feel like you're in a city anymore. So long as you look towards Mosman, away from the bridge. The water's edge—particularly the banyan trees, vines, rock pools, lazy fish with a view of high-rise—gives me an easy feeling. As if nature will always win. In the intimate inner suburbs, I love how the roads and paths are built along the lines of the fingers of rock that sweep down into the harbour. I like to imagine what the Aborigines would have felt looking for fish, going after the possums. And it occurs to me to pray for them, for all those souls known only to you. God, what did you think of them? In a way I'm living like them. There's too much in the past. Imagine all those people and where they end up. Prayer is always open-ended. You can't pray ironically, and you can't pray as if you are right. Prayer must always leave open the possibility that you are wrong. Prayer always says, maybe it is your fault for looking. And I'm sort of daydreaming in my zen state, praying for this groaning world when across the bay I see two—I shit you not, two lions, one male, one female—pacing and circling on the rocks just above the waterline. A whaler goes past without seeing them. They must have escaped from the zoo. I put my rosary around Prince's neck.

And then without even knowing it, I'm all wet and bobbing up and down trying to keep the shaggy mane in view, and then panting and holding the edge of the rock as the water surges around me. The male is looking at me from a big rock covered with orange lichen one level above me. I get up on the rock and start wringing out my clothes. The female lifts her head, eyeing me off, then curls up again. The sun beats down and I quickly dry off. To see these beasts up close is magnificent, although they do have a bit of a smell. We stare into each others' eyes. The male rests his head on his crossed paws.

I hear the beating of the Channel Seven chopper before I see it. It's on the same line of sight as the bridge. The lions roar up at it as it settles over us. Not that I can hear them, I can just see the male's jaws at full stretch. And then the next roar is so loud I can actually make it out over the chopper. They're sending down a ladder for me, God knows why. I gesture to them, indicating I'll swim back when I'm ready. The water is shimmering under the beating of the blade and the lions are so agitated they bound away over the rocks and into the trees.

"Keep your feet together," the man yells in my ear. The guy wraps his arms around me and as I'm hoisted up I see them between the gaps in the trees trotting along the footpath.

Back at the cop shop, the officer says there was nothing illegal in what I did, "just batshit."

"No fixed address," I say.

They took me to the hospital, but they couldn't decide whether to admit me because of you-know-what, so I just walked out as soon as no one was looking. Back at the Palace, Brice shows me the clip on his phone. It made me look like I was a hostage being rescued, but God would have never allowed those lions to harm me. COURAGEOUS RESCUE, said the tagline at the bottom of the screen. "You should be dead, mate." We have a good laugh over the clip. He says the presenter is doing a Masonic sign with her hands while she talks about me. Who the fuck knows, mate.

Just then, from the bottom of the Palace, Prince came sprinting, like I knew he would, but I wasn't expecting him so soon. What can I say? Christ is with me always. It can't be put into words. I don't want to put it into words. I read somewhere that words are a degeneration in culture, used only because ESP lost its force. Can always move in with Clay for a few months to get back on my feet. Tonight I will pray without ceasing, for everyone I ever knew, all of them, even that Arch.

# THE OLIVE PIT

When Janice agreed to marry me ten years ago, her one condition was that I give up active duty and take a desk job. At the time I was one of the best marksmen on the force, and at thirty-five I still had good years ahead of me. "I love you, honey, but I couldn't handle it if you killed someone in the line of duty or if I saw you on the news beating someone with a nightstick," she said. "Even if they deserved it a million times over, you'd be a monster to me."

We live, or used to live, on five and a half acres in the foothills, about ten minutes' drive from the station. The previous owners of our property raised racehorses. When we bought it, I converted the stable into a studio for Janice. I ripped out the stalls, bleached the floor, laid down hardwood, and installed insulation and double-paned skylights. Janice used the spectacular views of the valley and the Traverse Mountains as inspiration for most of her work.

Sometimes she painted a whole picture in just one day, in a trance, brush hand on the canvas, the other stretched out, palm up behind her like Tinkerbell. Her paintings were all over our walls. They still sell some of them as posters and postcards at the tourist centre. She said that the valley and the mountains changed every time she looked at them—brightness, colour, shadow—and eventually I came to see that too.

In 1989, after a nationwide manhunt, hydroponics specialist Jordan Depaul was found in the Salt Lake City house he'd barely left for years. He was convicted of the murder of five Dole Fruit truck-drivers between the years 1985 and 1987. God's work, he said. He had no regrets. It was the usual story: absent mother, bitter father, twisted personal religion. After he was sentenced to death, he pored over the criminal statutes and discovered that a forgotten writ permitted him to choose the firing squad instead of the customary lethal injection. Depaul's loophole was closed the next year, but it wasn't retroactive. His wish had to be carried out, and I volunteered for some of the carrying.

After ten years of shooting paper targets at the range, ten years of reading about robberies and on-duty deaths, even petty vandalism reports started to get my blood rushing. My brother was a typist in the Vietnam War and developed sympathetic post-traumatic stress disorder—even though he was never fired upon—transmuting his guilt at spending the war in an air-conditioned base. That guilt, fostered by typing up accounts of mutilation and death day after day, destroyed him. Maybe worse than if he'd actually fought himself. I understood him.

And I wanted to know what it felt like to shoot someone. Some of my colleagues had killed perpetrators in self-defense and it changed them, lent them a certain gravitas. Any man who tells you he's not envious, on some level, of men with combat experience is a liar. It sounds bad to say, but I couldn't let the opportunity pass me by. And what difference did it make if I did the shooting or not? Someone else would.

A week before the execution, Warden Jeffries gave the five of us a tour of the execution chamber. He showed us the whitewashed wall with a slit for us to shoot through and a mockup of the target that would be pinned over his heart: a white paper square with a black circle in the middle.

"Now, you all know this is highly unusual, and will probably never happen again. Your job is not to let it turn into a spectacle," he said.

He then explained the procedure we were to follow on the night. An unmarked van with no windows would pick us up at the police station at eleven and drive us to the prison. Before our arrival, our five rifles would be loaded with two rounds each. According to tradition, one of the rifles would contain two wax bullets, so there would always be the possibility that any one of us hadn't killed him. At five to midnight, we would be handed our weapons by an officer who had not seen them being loaded. We would enter the chamber and take our positions while the warden watched from the second level through one-way glass. Depaul would walk or, if unable to move under his own power, be escorted in and given two minutes to speak. The shooters would kneel behind their rifles and the squad captain—the role that fell to me, as the most senior volunteer—would whisper to each in turn to see if they were ready. Then the squad captain would give the ready signal to the warden, receive final confirmation from him through an earpiece, lower his rifle, and count down from five to one. Then we would fire.

My four deputies were Johnson, who exasperated his partner with his inexplicable silences on duty; Young, who lost his left ring finger to the knife of a heroin pusher in Liberty Wells; Kupeofola, an imposing, black-eyed Tongan; and Selwood, the serious one, who never broached a joke, about himself or anyone else. We had all scored perfect 75s at the range at least a dozen times and averaged above 72. Our identities were unknown to everyone but ourselves and the warden and, it must be emphasised, we all volunteered for the detail.

That week the five of us practiced with blanks at the range every day during our lunch break. Our goal was to fire simultaneously with one loud report instead of five scattered cracks. Accuracy was a given. From twenty feet you can't miss with a .30-30. When we started, we sounded like five cork pop guns competing for attention. By the day before the execution, we sounded like a cannon.

. . .

When I got home from work on the night before the execution, Janice was chopping onions. I could hear the sharp knock of the knife on the wood as I opened the front door. As always when she cooks, she had the radio on, and of course they were jabbering in concerned tones about the big execution. She is the only person I know who prefers radio to television. She said radio allows her to imagine a scene while television imposes one on her.

After I shook the snow off my boots, I came up behind her, wrapped my arms around her, and kissed the back of her neck. The sting of the onion caught my eyes, and I started to tear-up.

"What are you making?"

"Bolognese. As if you care so long as there's plenty of it." She cracked a handful of spaghetti in half and dropped it in the pot. The water hissed briefly. She turned down the radio. "They just said the attorneys aren't going to file any last-minute appeals. It's up to the parole board now."

"I doubt they'll issue a stay."

"Do you know any of the firing squad?"

"I've met them," I said.

She set out the bowls and slammed the steaming pot of pasta in the center of the table. As usual, I finished her leftovers. While we were eating dessert—mint chip ice cream—she asked, "Do you know what he asked for? For his last meal?"

"No." The warden had advised me not to watch TV or read the papers until it was over.

"An olive."

"Just an olive?"

"Just an olive. And he asked to be buried with the pit in his pocket."

I didn't know what to say, so I scooped up a spoonful of ice cream. In the silence my spoon clinked on the rim of the bowl.

She began again. "Why do you think he asked for that olive and nothing else?"

"Hmmm," I said. "I wouldn't want anything but this ice cream."

"It seems odd, doesn't it? Some kind of spiritual exercise, maybe? I can't see a political point being made with an olive."

"Maybe he's trying to invoke the olive branch of peace. Trying to tell us he's found inner peace."

"What would you know about inner peace?" she said with that teasing smile.

"More than him, I bet. What would you want for a last meal?" I asked.

"You," she said, and leaned over the table and kissed me. "Or five blocks of Valrhona dark chocolate."

* * *

The next morning, I woke up before dawn, primed and alert. At six I did my half hour on the treadmill, had a shower, then put my uniform and boots on. I forgot I didn't need to be at the station until eleven that night. I walked downstairs to the kitchen with a heightened sense of reality, that transcendent awareness that used to make me turn the patrol car down an alley on impulse to find a mugging in progress. Everything looked newly congealed. I fixed myself a cup of coffee and went over to the living room window. The soft blanket of snow outside had thickened overnight.

"What are you doing up this early?" Janice had come down silently in her pink slippers. I always liked how she looked in the mornings. She never took her pajamas off before noon and when she walked I'd catch hints of her firm legs and smooth hips as the material brushed against her skin.

"I don't know, just looking at the mountains. They aren't half as beautiful as those paintings by Janice Lee Draper. You heard of her?"

"Ain't she the wife of that handsome cop?"

"I believe so, yes. He sure is one lucky man."

"I thought you weren't working until tonight." She'd noticed my uniform. I'd told her I had the eight-to-two overnight dispatch shift.

"Uh, I don't know. I just forgot."

She laughed and gave me a little pat on the behind. "Well, put something else on and I'll get the pancakes ready."

I came back down in civilian clothes and sat down in front of five steaming pancakes.

"Mmm," I said, as I chewed, "these are good enough to be a last meal."

"Aren't you funny," she said. Then she became quiet, and I knew by the way she was cutting her pancakes, with exaggerated precision, that she was about to say something serious.

"You know, I had a dream about it last night. I was facing the firing squad. But no one put a hood on me, and I was trying to explain that I was the wife of a police officer. They had mistaken me for someone else. I screamed and screamed but they shot anyway. I didn't feel any of the shots and I still had all my senses. The bright lights were on me, and a doctor came and felt my wrist, and I tried to tell everyone that I was still alive but no sound would come out. And I was complaining that I didn't even get a last meal. Then I woke up."

"Always thinking about food, you." I chuckled a little, but she wasn't laughing. "What was your crime?"

"Nothing. I hadn't done anything."

"But they must have at least accused you of something?"

"I suppose they did, but I didn't know what it was."

After breakfast Janice went off to paint, so I drove to the batting cages in town. You can just put all your focus on counting the rhythm of the mechanical arm and smacking the ball as hard as you can.

After warming up in the seventy-five-mile-an-hour cage, I moved up to the eighty-five and was hitting nearly every ball into the back of the net. I was in a groove. Step, swing, pop. Step, swing, pop. Two eight or nine-year-olds came over to watch me, and after a particularly flat line drive, I heard one of them say, "Maybe he plays for the Bees."

The next pitch came out with no spin on the ball. The red stitches, two curves on the white, enlarged in slow motion as they rushed towards me. Before I could get out of the way, the ball hit the knuckle of my right index finger—my trigger finger—jamming it into the bat handle. For a second I felt nothing, and then it felt like my knuckle had been cracked in a vise. I'd never seen a worse pitch from a machine. Six seconds later the next pitch thudded into the canvas backstop, straight down the middle.

"If you rub it, you're a wimp," said one of the kids. "Do you play for the Bees?"

"No, but I'm flattered you asked."

I peeled my gloves off and walked back to the girl behind the counter, who clutched her phone between two thumbs, and said, "You should check the eighty-five machine. It just hit me on the hand."

She looked up. "Which one?"

"The eighty-five."

"We had them all serviced last week. No one else has complained."

"I'm not complaining. I should have been able to dodge it anyway. I just want to make sure it doesn't get anyone else."

"Well, I don't know what you want me to do then."

"Think if it hit someone in the head."

"I'll tell the manager when he gets back."

The two boys, having lost interest in me, were looking at the rare baseball cards laid out in individual cases underneath the glass countertop. Generosity sneaks up on me sometimes. Their parents probably dropped them off at the batting cages for the day because it was too cold to throw them outside. It might be hours before they were picked up again.

"Two packs of Topps, please," I said to the girl.

"Ten dollars."

I stretched out my hurt finger, which had begun to swell like a kielbasa, and opened my wallet with my thumb and middle finger.

"Hey," I said, "take one each."

They ripped open the foil packaging. "Thanks, Mister."

. . .

Twenty-three years of shooting have given me hands like gold-dust scales, and my rifle weighed not a gram under regulation.

Aside from the few eager souls at the prison gate waving blue glow sticks and holding hands and singing, the ride over had been silent. We waited in an anteroom for what seemed like a long time. I kept my gloves on so no one would see my injury. Small talk was difficult, but we did it anyway. It's funny, I still remember Selwood saying his daughter had pneumonia.

We stood behind the concrete wall as Depaul shuffled out unassisted. A lick of white hair stood up at the back of his head. It was hard to picture this wispy man as the brash murderer on TV from fifteen years before. He declined to speak. The guard asked if he understood that he had a right to speak. He said, "Yes, sir," then he was strapped to his wooden chair up on the wooden platform with black sand bags stacked all around to prevent ricochets.

His black hood was fitted. Then the target was pinned to his chest with two safety pins. His bonds were double-checked, and the guards withdrew. Perched between the black stacks, he reminded me of a statue in its niche. The others were ready. I knelt down on the right end and took my right glove off but kept my hand in front of me so the warden couldn't see from behind. I turned the safety off my rifle and put my finger, as tight and firm as a hose on full blast, pain barreling through it, on the outside of the trigger guard. I raised my left hand, giving the signal to the warden. "All clear, buddy," I heard him say. The paper target slowly turned into a baseball card, and I heard myself starting to count. Around two I remember thinking that the black now looked more like purple and the lights had brightened. I could barely make out the sandbags. I fainted somewhere before four with my finger on the trigger.

I don't remember my rifle going off or the recoil hitting my shoulder, but there was a bruise there the next day. When I came to, Kupeofola was shaking me from behind and three doctors were frantically undoing Jordan's bonds. Blood was dripping down his chair and onto the floor. My finger was in a crucible of pain. I sat up and wrapped my arms around my knees. My four deputies were staring at me with puzzled expressions. "What happened?" I asked.

"You hit him in the stomach," Selwood said.

They performed emergency surgery on Depaul that night. At two a.m. the warden decided I couldn't be charged with any crime, but I would have to present at the inquest. He drove me back to the station so I could get my car. I didn't go home straight away but drove around looking at the encircling Traverses in the three-quarter moon.

When I got home Janice was still up, painting in the sky-lit stable. "The moon is good tonight," she said. She kissed me. "How was work?"

"Quiet. It's too cold for criminals. Did you finish anything?"

"You're gonna laugh at me."

"No, I'm not."

"Yes, you will."

There on the canvas, in shades of ash and pale green, was an olive. The morning took a long time to arrive.

# YOUR EISENHOWER DOLLAR

The problem with your life is this: if a gun is ever going to be put to your head, today is the most likely day. And on Vasconcelos Street just outside metro Juanacatlán, it happens.

You reach for the gun. But then you are calm and follow the constellation of white-shirted pilgrims calling and responding to each other, out of the metro station past the food carts and the cross-legged beggar with a snake and a cup for change in front of him, down the long avenue lined with American fast-food outlets, Oxxos, and souvenir shops, towards the spires of the basilica.

"Puerta," you say to yourself as you walk through the gate. Like a boulder in a stream, you pass through the pilgrims. Their words are meaningless to you. As they file into the circular New Basilica, you are left alone facing the kneeling gothic facade of the Old Basilica.

The Eisenhower dollar in your pocket clings to your leg in the heat. You had found twenty of them, matted and scuffed from use, fitting snug in a Maggi beef bouillon tube, in a box in your grandfather's house, among Morgans, silver dimes, wheat pennies, and silver proof sets from 1963 to 2013, the year he died, this year. On the Internet you learned that the Ikes weren't worth much. Even uncirculated specimens were selling for only a dollar-fifty. Ikes were rarely used in everyday commerce, except in the Nevada slot machines. Nineteen are gone, given to friends and family you had stayed with or as birthday presents to small cousins. You want to leave the remaining coin somewhere symbolic to reflect your new beliefs.

The sign in front of the Old Basilica says: no sunglasses, no hats, no shorts, and no noise. You are starting at a disadvantage: you are wearing shorts. But they will know you are a tourist. Backpack, sunglasses, height. Solitary. Surely you won't be kicked out. The trouble is that you want them to know that the basilica, for you, is not just a destination to be checked off a list.

Your curiosity began one long-forgotten day when you were struck cold with the thought that the idea which you had heard without reservation in so many different versions—that a human being could decide for himself what was right or wrong, good or bad, evil or gracious, beneficial or detrimental—was nonsense. It was the same as saying "jabba wabba ding dong" or "supercalifragilisticexpialidocious." But then what was to decide for you? And in making that choice weren't you faced with the same fundamental absurdity, you thought, though not in those precise terms? Again you became a child with interminable whys. Why is it wrong to kill someone? But why, but why? Revelation in some form, you decided, was necessary.

When you were a child, your parents had taken the family to church—Anglican—every once in a while, mostly at Easter and Christmas, but occasionally throughout the year. Your mother and your sister sometimes sang in the church choir and your most prominent memory of church is sitting in the front row next to a friend of your mother's, holding a paper sign that said, "Hi Mom." You also remember the Bach recessionals and a fear of baptism, which came about because, watching the baptism of babies, you assumed you would also need to be naked at the front of church.

It had continued with books. *The Power and the Glory* in high school had captivated you, and then on it went. It seemed to happen with increasing frequency. Similar to the way, as a child, you always seemed to encounter forty-four minutes past the hour on digital clocks, you would enjoy a book or a poem, or a friend would recommend an author and invariably, when you researched the authors, they would turn out to be Catholics or former Catholics or deathbed penitents like Wallace Stevens. This slow revelation of your preferences led you to apologetics, Chesterton, St. Augustine. You agreed with Alasdair MacIntyre when you could parse him (your twelfth-grade English teacher recommended him) but stopped reading *After Virtue* halfway through.

The Bible was good too. You had started reading at least a page a night, occasionally more if the story gripped you, and you prayed, but your own prayers. You thanked God for the blessings of the day, which was a little silly, but you tried not to be grateful for material things, but more for safety and communion with friends or family. Then you asked to be forgiven of your sins, and without knowing what else to do you ran through the seven deadlies and any specific transgression, usually a lie or an act of rudeness you had committed that day. You also prayed for specific others. Your boss's wife had miscarried a much-anticipated baby, and you prayed for your boss and his wife and the "unborn soul" of the fetus. Then you asked for "the power and courage to perceive and live in reality, which is yours alone," a phrase you had formulated yourself but must have read somewhere. Finally the Lord's Prayer and swift sleep. Though you would have liked to have told someone you were doing this, you did not. You did not go back to a church or approach a priest. You justified this by telling yourself you would not treat church like a self-help regimen. You told yourself to wait until you moved out of your parents' house, until you got a girlfriend, a salaried job, decent savings. The trip to Mexico City cut your Bible reading short at the death of Moses.

Your sister lives in Mexico City. She did not come home to Costa Casa for your grandfather's funeral a few weeks ago, and your mother is worried about her. Your mother paid for your flight as a graduation present. Your sister took Advanced Placement Spanish as a junior in high school, aced the test, and enrolled at UNAM. When you meet her friends in a bar near the university, one of them says she didn't suspect Louisa wasn't Mexican for years, not until she heard Louisa put strange emphases into the word "Teotihuacan." You haven't seen your sister for nearly four years; you have barely spoken. Her ex-boyfriend had somehow found her Gmail password and deleted or blocked—you were never sure which—messages from her friends and family. The door of her tiny room brushes the bed when it opens. The two of you can't avoid sleeping in each other's arms. She tells you about the breakup.

"We went to this club and there was this DJ from England and I requested a song from him in English and just chatted for a bit and Juan blew up—said I didn't love him and why don't I go suck the British guy's dick—and I just left and sat in the park and he came and found me and was like, look what a good boyfriend I am, you would have been attacked if I hadn't found you and I'm sorry and let's forget it. So I went back with him. I had nowhere else to go and then he took my key away and started crying again and told me to leave and go fuck the British guy, so I said fine and opened the window. The apartment was on the eighth floor. I sat on the windowsill and thought, why should I die, he should die, oh Nathan, why is it so serious? So I got a knife and stabbed him. Just a butterknife. He didn't even bleed."

"And then?"

"The neighbours called the cops and, yeah, it was like a proper domestic."

"Yeah, you'd probably die from the eighth floor."

"And he kept Pirata, our dog."

Love turns the loved one supernatural and you think about the difference between the iconic and the idolatrous. An icon is a mnemonic device, an idol is a death sentence. He made for himself an idol out of Louisa and what he knew of generosity and destroyed her as idols are destroyed. You remember him from when she had brought him back one Christmas. You had gone to Knott's Berry Farm with them and he had been afraid of the rides and made Louisa wait with him, leaving you alone in the two or four-seat cars.

"So, anything else exciting happen in the last four years?" you ask.

"Mmm, oh yeah, we got mugged. In the middle of the day."

"Where?

"Just walking down the street this guy pulled out a gun, but the thing is, Juan Alberto jumped in front of me, like instinctively. Yeah, he was controlling, but he was also going to protect me."

"How much got stolen?"

"Like, a hundred pesos. I wasn't scared while it was happening. But later I was like, oh my God, what if his finger slipped or something. Don't tell Mom, ever."

You discuss going to the basilica, how to use the metro, which stops to avoid. Religion comes up. She tells you she crossed her fingers underneath the hymn book when the choir sang statements of belief. Later she made up her own religion involving Egyptian gods and a dead wasp that was stuck in her curtains. She held a rite for the wasp to assuage her guilt. "Are you a Catholic now?" she asks, laughing. "Mom said you read lots of Catholic books."

"Sort of. I've started praying."

"You'll get over it. You're just a bit out of it. You need a job and a girlfriend and you'll be fine."

"Don't, Louisa."

"Okay, God will save you, whatever. I'm doing research on how the brain is stimulated the same way by meditation and prayer."

"Dad's started doing yoga at this resort in Laguna Beach. He pretends to be a guest so he can get free coffee and go to the free class on Saturday mornings."

"Haha, you can pray and meditate with me and then tell me how you feel after each."

Before you fall asleep you feel that giddy fatigue that feels like salvation, like you couldn't be asked for anything more. Eventually a dream comes to you. Anthony Hopkins floats across a bed towards a sleeping woman in a chair. He stares at you and says "Hell." He is going to kill the woman in the chair. He has already tucked one neatly underneath the bed. And the cups on your tray have been turned upside down. You wake up and wonder if you have fought off a demon trying to possess you. "Dear Lord, protect me from the corrosive acids of self-pity, protect me from false congratulation, protect me from the corruption of self-loathing." After breakfast you take Louisa's metro card and your Ike dollar and depart for the basilica.

. . .

Inside the Old Basilica a painting of Pope Saint Pius X catches your eye. All you know about him is the society founded in protest of Vatican II. Truth be told, you like knowing these sorts of facts—the categories and factions, which saint is for which purpose—more than knowing justifications of doctrine or prayers or even the stories of Christ. You are more interested in reading about inquisitorial procedure, miracles of the saints, autos-da-fé, and Vatican intrigue, than in examining your own actions. You consider throwing the Ike in the donation box, but you think they might not know what it is, or someone might think it's valuable and take it.

You remember your grandfather's funeral at the sharp-cornered church in Indiana with the wooden cross in front of the wooden pews, the thin blue carpet and white walls and the hum of the humidifier. The memory contrasts with the ordered opulence of gold and pink and blue in the basilica. You are seduced by the red and gold, the tormented bodies, outstretched arms, reclining padres, stained-glass murals, the icons of the Old Basilica.

You sit down in a pew near the back. An old man and an old woman, a peasant couple, crawl on their knees into the pew and sit next to you. A young woman, probably their granddaughter, walks in behind them. The granddaughter assists the older couple onto the hassocks but does not kneel herself. The old people cross themselves with a cross made from their first and middle fingers. An itch begins at the hairline on your forehead. Come on, this is ridiculous. You want to ask the old peasant why she believes, what the Virgin means to her, why she crosses herself, why she prays, why she crawls on her knees, and you hope she cannot answer. You hope those questions would be incomprehensible to her. Convert or not, you would never feel that. It could only be felt as much as a sleeper feels the blanket. You want to ask her what God feels like, but you do not have the Spanish. The hassock lays there below you. The two old people finish praying. Just wait for them to leave, you think, then kneel. The couple return to their feet and pull the hassock up. Not meant to be. You leave without kneeling.

You walk to the New Basilica and move through the circular building, catching a Spanish word every now and then. The cadence of the Lord's Prayer, unmistakable in any language, resounds from the priest's microphones and the mouths of hundreds of pilgrims, signalling the end of Mass. You hurry out so as not to be caught in the crowd and head up the stairs to Tepeyac Hill. You sit down on a stone wall and look down to the square, the gate, the avenue, and the city beyond. The man sitting a few meters away turns to you.

"You speak English?" he asks.

"Yes."

"So am I. Why you come here, you are Catholic?"

"Sort of?"

"What do you mean?"

"I like it, but I don't go to church often."

"Like me. Lots of you around."

You find out his name is Juan. He is a refugee from Cuba. He has been in Mexico City for a week, under interrogation, with a final hearing tonight at six. He says he was a medic in the army and that he has been to Angola, Zimbabwe, Somalia. He has scars on his face. He said he had to flee Cuba because he emailed some beach photos to a friend in America. How did he make a friend in America? On a medical assignment in Namibia, he says.

It doesn't sound right, he must have done more than that, you think, but his presence is enjoyable, he is not asking for help, and he allows you to stop thinking of yourself. Your conversation turns into subtle tests of knowledge in which you find that you are roughly equal and that he is not sensitive. "When the metro first opened, peasants would flag down the train like a bus then line up at the front car to board. It stopped every time." You think about giving him your coin, but it would be no use to him, and you are afraid of offending him. "You know people here," he says. "In Coyoacan, the Condessa, they think they are rich. They will get a surprise if they go to the United States. They will be nothing. You know Porfirio Diaz, the dictadura, made all this. Dictadura, is still happening."

"Yes, I know Porfirio Diaz."

A girl sitting a few yards away approaches you and Juan. She asks in English if either of you know how to play chess. Juan defers to you. The heavily shadowed eyes of Kurt Cobain look out from the girl's t-shirt. She has on a black bowler hat. Her hair is streaked with blond. You notice a worn paperback by J. D. Salinger with a Spanish title inside her handbag. "This is what the man who shot John Lennon was reading, so I thought, let's see." You can tell she is attracted to you, and you want to find out how old she is so you can invite her to Louisa's party.

"Why did you come here?" you ask.

"My parents believe and take me to church sometimes, but I just think it's very beautiful here. I had the day off school."

"I was wondering. If no one believed in God, would he exist? If I don't believe in God, does he exist? Am I God? Do I exist?" Juan says.

You begin playing chess with Esther. Juan and Esther chat in Spanish and then bring you in with English, light topics. You win the chess match easily, and she sets up the board again. What is the age of consent in Mexico? You are certain it is below eighteen. You can't remember feeling so unconcerned about the future as at this moment. It starts to rain. The three of you move into the small shelter offered by the umbrella of the icon stand. Esther asks you for a piece of paper and writes down a couple of Mexican songs for you to look up. She moves away with haste through the rain, clutching her bag to her chest, back to her parents. Juan smiles to the distance. You say farewell to Juan.

You descend the hill by the back staircase. A water hose gushes into one of the gardens. An Indian woman is filling bottles with the water and as she does you can see the yellow taint of the water. The dollar digs into your finger. It would be useless to her, and perhaps demeaning to receive it, but she, another human, needs it more than the basilica does, and the symbolism couldn't be beat: an Eisenhower dollar, saved from the maw of Vegas, redeemed in the hands of a pious Nahua grandmother.

"Hola, ¿cómo estás?" you say brightly, holding out the coin. "Please take this," you say in English under your breath.

She doesn't move at first then puts the hose down with care, grasps the coin, and stares it down. "No sé, no es Mexicano." She hands the coin back to you. "Gracias." You do not insist.

Eisenhower wrote a letter the night before D-Day taking responsibility if the operation failed. You have a fancy of Eisenhower coins circulating through the slots and chutes of casinos, bleeding out occasionally in the tray of some retiree, that face always in motion. Towards the end of his life your grandfather went to Vegas twice a year. Something about the Parkinson's drove him to gambling. He couldn't be faulted; he never lost more than he could afford. The proof is in the Ike you stroke as you walk up to the Antiqua Parroquia de los Indios.

In the right nave of the Parroquia, Juan Diego lived and tended the Virgin for the rest of his mortal days. His room has sunk well below the modern church floor, and iron bars prevent people from falling in. You approach the anchorage with your fingers around the Ike. The ground is littered with coins, letters, and paper money— mostly Mexican but also Yankee, European, and Central American.

Candles flicker in their midst. You reflect that a fire could easily start with a stray banknote. You throw your one and two-peso coins into Juan Diego's anchorage. Tears begin to form behind your eyes but do not fall. It is the same feeling that happens occasionally when you are alone watching TV and a story about a handicapped child or a grieving mother comes on the news. Most people would call you a calm, even-keeled, even cold person, and in truth you are. Your lapses in the face of audiovisual stimulation don't change that. "Jesus Christ, this is spectacular," you say to yourself and instantly, "Stop saying that, not here, not now."

You come to the low iron fence surrounding a fountain where a group of gargantuan dark-skinned statues stand in the water and act out Juan Diego's revelation. The Virgin is painted in the same gaudy, fluorescent colours as the cloak. The rest are their original, almost-black, metal, with swathes of colour on their loin-cloths and headscarves. It starts to rain. You bring out your dollar coin and hold it by the edge. The sound of rain muffles the sound of Ike hitting the water, and you do not see the coin floating on towards the statues.

Past the long avenue, which is busier now than in the morning. The beggar's snake has bitten a woman, but she is okay. The snake is not venomous, and the man offers her the contents of his cup with a smile. You walk back down the steps into the metro station. "Moneda," the man had said. It had sounded odd to refuse, odder still to lunge for the gun.

If you did not develop extravagant tastes or severe illness, you could have lived your whole life without struggle at home in Costa Casa, greeted Fernando the barista at the coffee shop, walked to work, taken girls to the top of lifeguard towers at Corona del Mar, inherited your parents' houses, invested in stocks and silver, accrued mystical poetry in the bottom drawer of your desk, and died surrounded by three of your four children in a hospital room with a view of the mountains and the ocean. A fine life, but you craved judgment.

While you wait on the platform, you look down at the tracks and you don't see the words scrolling along the news ticker: The Ministerio de Relaciones Exteriores today denied asylum to Juan Diego the Cuban refugee. Esther's father has been sentenced to fifteen years in prison for embezzling half a billion pesos from the Department of Transport. Nathan Litterbach of Costa Casa, California, found dead on Avenida Maestro José Vasconcelos in the Condessa on Thursday. The ticker, when you finally look up at the screen, reads: "Jueves 18-25, lluvia."

# SHROVE TUESDAY

My coconut flour pancakes were a failure. Although I had followed the recipe in *I Can't Believe It's Not Gluten* to the letter, somehow my mix would not blend. My mixing cup was half cloudy liquid on top, a thin strip of good batter in the middle, and sludge on the bottom. The experimental pucks in the pan (cooked in coconut oil) had turned to charred mush.

"Oh, I'm so sorry," gloated Father O'Riordan, who had wearied of my pontificating about the threat to the human body of drought-resistant wheat, soil depletion, pesticides, gut irritation, and similar depredations of industrial food production. "You'll just have to have the old-fashioned ones."

It was all right for him to talk; he wasn't looking for a wife.

So I was grateful that the rectory kitchen was such a bustle, with air-con at full blast. No one except Father really took notice. There were half a dozen other mixing bowls on the table along with bags of flour, sugar, glistening waves of butter, a nearly empty bottle of maple syrup, three types of honey, a small plate of lemon zest, and goat's cheese. Despite the heat the oven was on to char the palm leaflets for the next morning's Mass. I had cut them that morning from the tree in the backyard.

Father O'Riordan's friend, Eleanor, who had just landed from England, expertly flipped pancakes and set them out browned to perfection in a stack at the centre of the table. She flipped the top two and heaped them with syrup and banana pucks then set the plate down in front of Father. He had told me that she wanted to marry him thirty years earlier when he was in England. "But there was no chance of that," he had said in his droll way. "But she's very generous. Her husband died and left her stacks. You don't know the half of what she funds around here."

"Her husband, you mean the second choice after you?"

"We're not going there."

Donna, the parish treasurer, and her husband Paul poured cups of tea and glasses of wine for the seven or eight middle-aged parishioners squeezed into the kitchen. My conversations with them followed the same lines—surface concerns—job (between), car (yes, for now), study (on hiatus)—conversations as boring as the nightly news, but where else was there to go?

In Australia, Easter most often falls at the beginning of autumn. It's all wrong. Symbolically, I mean. It can be anywhere from frosty to warm on Easter Day, but it almost always marks the beginning of the end of the hot weather and the descent into winter. Shrove Tuesday falls at the end of summer when Melbourne becomes a steam room.

In defeat I placed my useless pan in the sink and went to answer the doorbell.

Jesse was at the door holding a bag of flour.

"Is this the fat day?" he said.

"Fat Tuesday, yes."

Although I did not yet know him well, I was glad to see another face from my generation. Jesse was a type I knew we would be getting more of. I remembered how he looked like death warmed up at the first Sunday in the parish hall after Mass. I felt it was my unique purview in some sense to welcome these types. I was like them but more psychologically stable. He had just dropped out of a mathematics PhD and was driving the catering van for his father's Italian restaurant.

"I'm just an absolute wretch," he said, leaning back in his chair. "We should abolish numbers. It should be one, two, three, many, that's it."

I told him about a friend's father I had just met, a physics professor who was calculating the weight of the universe. In fact, his team had just received a twenty-million-dollar grant from the government for this purpose. I had asked him what the use of the information would be, and he couldn't say. Jesse laughed when I told him this, and I think it made him feel like he could trust me.

After a few minutes of glancing at each other as the older folk caroused and ate their pancakes, I suggested we go for a walk, to which he hungrily agreed.

Although the clock said early evening, outside the sun was blazing. As we walked and our initial small talk concluded, he said, "I'm such a wretch. It's that thing."

"Which thing?"

"You know, *that* thing."

"Yes, of course."

"It's the phone. If we didn't have phones, it wouldn't be a problem. I just want to go to church, do my woodworking, pray. No internet, no technology."

"I've convinced myself that Donna can see all the history. She handles all the rectory bills."

"Yeah, that's good."

"I'm actually at more than two hundred days."

"I'm at, uh, eighty."

"Fantastic, that's great."

"Uh, minutes."

"Oh."

"No one tells you it's bad. My Mum would buy those magazines for my brother and me when we were, like, fourteen."

"It's so difficult, mate, it's the hardest thing to give up."

Unconsciously, I was walking towards the pocket park behind the basketball courts where I did my morning reading. A five-storey apartment building overlooked the park and on the wall behind the basketball goals was a mural of an upside down wattle bird lunging at a magenta bottle-brush. We sat down on the back of a bench, feet on the seat, under a gazebo with a public barbecue.

"I'm at the point now where to find out what to think I ask my secular progressive friends and think the opposite," Jesse said.

"I know what you mean. Not the best way to make decisions, though."

"No, of course not, but then how?"

"You just have to know, you have to discern."

And then we saw it. There was a sign on the brick barbecue that read, "WARNING HOT SURFACE." It was a wooden sign, a relic from a less technocratic age, and the lettering had been scored an inch deep into the wood in strong rounded capitals. The word WARNING had been left au naturel, as it were, but HOT SURFACE had been filled in with pale yellow paint. In between WARNING and HOT SURFACE were the words NO GOD written in black Texta. WARNING NO GOD HOT SURFACE.

Jesse pulled a ballpoint pen out of his pocket and with feverish strokes made the letters K and W on either side of the NO until the lettering matched the width of the Texta lines.

"Nice."

Here I should say that Jesse was average height, with short black hair and a deep Sicilian complexion. He had a lumbering way of moving, like a rock star on stage or like he was in a rocking chair.

"How's life in the rectory?" he asked.

"Good."

"Is it good going to daily Mass?"

"Mate, it's the best thing. I know I probably won't do it forever, but it just focusses everything down, you know."

"You mean up?"

"Yeah lol, obviously."

"I don't know how my friends do it. Live, I mean. Where do they find meaning?"

I didn't reply right away. I was drinking in the heat. I decided it was safe to be earnest with him.

"It's sort of a paradox, right? Meaning can only be made on earth in terms of life everlasting. If it's oblivion at the end then nothing we do matters. Yet eternity itself, if you really think about it, can't be other than hellish. The prospect of eternity gives our actions meaning, but at the same time in eternity no action has any meaning. It's like that Borges story, "The Immortals," where these immortal men just lie around doing nothing. One of them falls down a canyon and they take hundreds of years to get around to rescuing him. That kind of thing. You could say, well, heaven is just completely beyond our comprehension, but I don't like that answer. How can we strive for it unless we have some inkling of what it might be like?"

"So, we're just completely bitched then."

"No, because that would make our creator evil."

"It's like those atheists who say a child with leukemia disproves God, or anyway a loving God, whereas it's just as easy to say that only a loving God could make sense of something like that. It's ultimately about your assumptions and what you most want. I think people largely get what they most want after death."

"Kierkegaard says we're always wrong before God."

"Obviously."

"Fuck it, then."

"Yes."

I was about to answer when we heard the bell ringing for evening prayer. Three tolls of three, then nine. We entered the Lady Chapel just as they finished singing the Angelus.

The first time I went to evening prayer, I wasn't expecting anything. It was a cold night, a Friday. I was completely overwhelmed. Father softly offering the petitions, placing the slips of paper on the chair beside him after each one—the cancers, the chronic illnesses, the degenerative diseases, the pleas for the conception of children, for family members to return to the Church, the welfare of imprisoned loved ones, the souls of the dead, the rare successes ("we give thanks for Seymour's remission")—all with names attached. Names of people I knew a bit from around the church, people I knew to be useful and cheerful, people who had just enjoyed pancakes in the rectory kitchen, revealed to be bearing intolerable burdens. If you think this is kitsch and sentimental, you're right.

Tonight it was Madeleine with her infected hip socket. While mostly focussing on praying, I was watching Jesse out of the corner of my eye. He sat slumped over the entire time, head in his hairy hands, legs wide, elbows on his knees.

As we exited the relative cool of the Lady Chapel into the furnace of the night, Jesse asked, "Beers? It's Shrove Tuesday, so we're morally obligated to get pissed."

"Yeah, we're doing no alcohol for Lent in the rectory so probably a good idea. I'll meet you at the park as soon as I get changed. I need to wear long sleeves and pants for the mosquitoes."

"I'll go to the shop and grab some."

When I arrived at the gazebo, Jesse handed me a bottle of Furphy.

"Not Furphy, bro."

"It was on special."

"I'm not drinking lies."

He grabbed my bottle and turned both his and mine over, allowing the liquid to drain completely out onto the concrete.

"Good idea. We'll get something else," he said, dumping the remaining four full bottles from the six-pack in the recycling bin.

As I jumped down from the bench, I saw it again. It was that same lettering in the same black Texta. The city council was trying hard to fit in with the geist of the suburb by posting its rules and regs in graffiti stencil form, like teenagers used to do with their favourite bands. One of these had been sprayed on the broad pillar of the gazebo. "Keep your dog on a leash" below a stencil figure of a person with a dog. This had been modified to read "Keep your GOD on a leash." Had it been there before? I was fairly certain it hadn't.

"Now he's just asking for it," Jesse said.

"Let's get some beers."

"Who's doing this?"

"Probably some high school boy. It's good, shows they're at least engaged."

"I guess it's more likely for someone like that to convert. Probably. Maybe."

"Definitely."

At the supermarket we got two six-packs of St. George's Premium Lager then returned to the scene of the crime. On a warm evening like this, of which plenty of light remained, the park would have been packed with little groups of friends on towels or blankets, drinking chilled wine or beer, kicking the footy or throwing tennis balls to their dogs, and even a few kids running around. But it was Tuesday, so we had the place to ourselves. I looked up at the apartment balconies behind us. It was a new build, a dogbox of glass and concrete. It would have been hell without air-conditioning on the top floors. I had lived in a similar building around the corner when I first came to the city. The lights were just starting to come on in those apartments, and I wondered if we were being watched. I couldn't make out any human shapes on the balconies or the windows. As the sun fell, mosquitoes began to bite my forehead and the back of my neck.

"Two hundred days, man what's that like?"

"Good, mate. I feel so level-headed, very grounded. Obviously, it's not easy."

"But Donna checks the history, remember."

"I've really convinced myself she does."

We were still side by side on the back of the bench when he spoke without looking in my direction:

"No one tells you it's bad, my Mum bought those magazines for me and my brother."

"You said that."

"It's all so backward. I remember when I was eight or so, my Mum would bring her boyfriends back. And my brother and I . . . went in to the living room and would ask, 'Are you okay, Mum?'"

I didn't know what to say.

He continued, "It's not inherently bad, the faculty itself. It's just disordered, the way it is now, in a place like this."

"Yeah."

He put down his empty bottle and opened another.

"We should try to catch this no-God loser. Let's get some food and stake out at the end of the wall."

It was almost too late. We got to the food court just as it was closing. Only the fast Mex was still serving. I realised I hadn't had anything to eat since breakfast, except a handful of coconut mush and two and a half beers—the half tucked away hidden in my left pocket, the mouth of the bottle under my shirt as I ordered a burrito bowl.

We ate and drank as we walked.

"My girlfriends always break up with me when they realise I'm only looking for Mumma."

"They always put too much lettuce on these, don't you think?"

"We're not rabbits."

"You know how kids don't like vegetables?"

"Yes."

"Well, what if that's because vegetables are bad for you, and they know by intuition?"

"Perfect, definitely true."

A few steps later we reached the corner of the park where the basketball courts met the parking lot fence. There was a small landscaped area with juvenile Manna Gums surrounded by bushes. I slid down against the wall behind a bush, and Jesse slid in beside me.

"How do you know he'll come back?"

"Shh, he's an atheist. He'll be back."

"We're just assuming it's a 'he'?"

"Lol."

"What are we going to do when we catch him?"

"Burn him at the stake. I don't know, mate. Dob him in for vandalism."

"You think they would press charges? Probably give him a medal instead."

I looked up again at the apartments. Only three were lit up now. The harshness of the lights in the parking lot intruded on my right and now very buzzed eye. The heat was still overbearing, with some slight breezes tickling the ends of leaves. Insect sensations and phantom insect sensations were running up my arms and my partially exposed lower back. My drooping posture was making leaning against the wall uncomfortable, so I moved into a crouch. That didn't last long either and it was back and forth leaning and sitting up, trying to keep my muscles from betraying me. It had also crossed my mind that Jesse could have done the graffiti himself. If the "Please Keep Your God on a Leash" hadn't been there already . . . then it was most likely him.

"Just two dudes hanging out in the bushes," Jesse said, "totally normal."

"Shhh."

And then I saw him. He was walking across the parking lot, seemingly unbothered by the light, walking slowly towards the entrance to the park—in other words, directly towards us. He was average height with a shaved head, somehow bulky without being either fat or toned, walking in a plodding, almost robotic way, while still seeming limber and keeping a good pace. He had on a black singlet, heavy black pants, black boots and—what made me freeze— what looked like a black surgical mask covering his mouth and nose. He continued lumbering right past our bush, just a few feet away, and to the gazebo.

"That's him," I whispered. "Has to be."

We could see him slowly moving around the gazebo.

"Fuck it, I'm sick of this."

Jesse stood up.

"Get down!" I whispered. "He'll see you."

Jesse brushed some wood chips off his pants and stepped around the bush into the glow of a streetlight.

"Hey! Are you the atheist?" he called out, hands cupped around his mouth to amplify the sound.

The figure took off running, away from us past the children's playground.

"Hey come back!" Jesse called. "Wanna beer?"

At that moment he turned the corner of the apartment building and was lost to our view.

At the gazebo he had added UN to cancel out Jesse's KN and make UNKNOW GOD. Not knowing how to add to this, Jesse just wrote I HEART GOD above it, in the same rapid strokes with his ballpoint pen.

"See you tomorrow for Ash Wednesday?" I said, "Eight a.m."

"Oh yeah, big time."

Back at the rectory Father O'Riordan and Eleanor were sitting across from each other drinking chilled white wine under the A/C outlet.

"What have you boys been up to?"

"Just preparing for Lent."

"That's good."

I was up with the bells for Mass and kneeling down next to Jesse as Father O'Riordan thumbed the cold black sludge on my pounding forehead.

# THREE VISIONS OF THE BEAN-NIGHE

Bean-nighe (Scottish): *a female spirit in the
form of a washerwoman, omen of death.*

*The First Vision*

She wore the pioneer dress to surprise him. It was a two-piece
that went down to her ankles, red-dotted with tiny white flowers
underneath and a white smock over the top, full sleeves with ruffles
at the ends. With her white bonnet and basket full of cured meat
and cheese hanging off her arm, she could have just stepped out of
a McCubbin.

"It's a dead shack," he told her. "There's no electricity, no running
water—just a tank—a firebox and an outhouse with a beehive under
the seat."

"No radiation, no phone service?"

"No phone service."

"And you'll make a fire?"

"I'll make a fire."

"I'm going to make a cake in your fire."

"Wonderful."

They drove out from Brunswick early on Tuesday morning to
beat the traffic. The winter sun rose slowly behind them, gradually
warming the day. As he drove, he fingered the ring in his jacket
pocket. It was his mother's engagement ring, three emeralds and
three diamonds of equally small size set in a gold band. This was the

trip he was going to ask her to marry him. In the morning everything would be magnificent. They would walk down to the wreck on the rocks at the edge of the bay and he would kneel down with the ring box in front of the rusty spire—facing the sea, of course. He knew never to turn his back to the waves to avoid being swept away. The light, the spray, the rocks—the photos.

The shack belonged to his grandmother, who was approaching her hundredth birthday in a nearby care facility, but only his aunt used it, visiting every few months to clear the driveway of wattle and rip out the invasive plants that threatened to overrun the natives along the creek. The block was not quite eighty acres, intersected by two creeks. There was one small property between it and the rocky beach. The shack sat on the peak of a gentle slope that tapered up to the far corner of the property. From the window and, even better, from the top of the concrete water tank that dominated the front of the shack, there were views of the hilly peninsula that bounded out into the strait.

They stopped at a pie shop in a small mangrove town—the place they always stopped when he was a kid on the way down, that advertised fifty different varieties of pie on the road-facing wall—and sat on the pier eating their pies and drinking chocolate milk while the crabs below them slow-danced in the mud.

After the mangrove town they passed a new housing tract and a shopping centre with Kmart and Big W. "This was just a country town when I was a kid," he said.

"It's so sad," she replied.

As they drove through green hills and dairy farms, as glimpses of the blue of the ocean gleamed through the scrub, he told her about his memories of the place: the family reunions, the picnics, his grandmother's eightieth birthday, when she was still *compos mentis*, the snakes, driving the tractor that his grandfather used to clear a path through the ferns and scrub to the beach. Further into the country, he showed her when to look to the right at the trestle rail bridge to glimpse the breakers spraying white foam high into the air under the wooden spars.

He missed the concealed driveway to the property, though, so they had to drive through the campground on the beach to turn around. Because it was the off-season there were no tents or caravans, except at one site, where Scott was surprised to see five green Army surplus tents around a campfire. A white minibus was parked nearby with a lyrebird logo Scott didn't recognise. No one seemed to be at the campsite.

As he began to painstakingly maneuver the car around in a five-point turn, something thudded against the passenger window. She screamed and then laughed. A red and blue Melbourne Demons football bounced back towards the scrub and two dusky-skinned boys chased after it. She rolled down the window and waved at the kids.

They stared and waved slowly back.

"Sorry," one of them said.

"That's all right," she said. "Look, Scotty, so cute."

"Yes."

"I didn't know there were Aborigines around here."

"Me neither."

The two boys resumed kicking the ball over the car as Scott turned the car around and slowly drove back away from the beach looking for the elusive driveway.

"They're funny," he said.

"They're cute."

. . .

On the windowsill of the shack were the same sheep and roo skulls he remembered, the same tiny bat skeletons, same dried sea sponge, and the quoll and wallaby carvings given to his grandfather by Aboriginal people of the Pilbara when he had been a flying doctor out of Dampier. On the walls were his uncle's drawings and paintings, all abstract, some of them well-achieved and others little more than scribbles.

He told her the story about the carvings that he told to every visitor. After his grandfather died his uncle, in a fit of guilt, wanted to send the carvings back to the people who gave them. They wrote back in polite but strong terms saying that to return a gift like that was extremely offensive in their culture.

"This is where the snakes will be, if there are any." He opened the door to the back shed that was next to the three double beds lining the back wall. There was no floor through the open door, just open white sand and the red tractor and a few cast-off machines and implements.

They walked down the creek, and he pointed out to her all the places from his childhood. "I used to crawl down those wombat holes with my grandmother. We'll do the wreck walk tomorrow. You can still see the metal parts of the hull sticking up. We used to go there all the time when I was a kid." He showed her the big heart carved into a tall Manna gum with eight straight deep cuts. His grandmother had told him it was there when she and his grandfather bought the place, and no one knew who had carved it. She twirled around under the heart and threw her arms around him. As they kissed, he wondered if maybe this was a better place for the proposal than the wreck. What a delightful problem to mull over tonight, he thought.

They returned to the shack through the fields of knee-high fern, stepping gingerly in case of snakes. Outside the shack he began chopping up a fallen bough for firewood. A smile fixed itself to her face as she watched him chopping, sweating and panting.

The winter sun was dying as he lit the fire. Soon, the shack was bathed in warmth, and condensation formed on the windows. She prepared the cake, wrapped the baking tin with foil, pushed the flaming logs to one side with the fire poker, and placed the tin on the thick layer of ash in the clearing she had made. It was a gluten-free, coconut-flour, dark chocolate cake, sweetened with honey and coconut sugar.

When she was done, they lay entangled on the couch and let the day slip away. It was fully dark by the time he said, "I'm going to drive into town and get dinner. Do you want to come? I might be a while."

"No, I'll keep an eye on the cake."

"Okay, Bean, I'll be back."

When the door closed behind him and the blast of cold air had been dominated by the heat of the fireplace, she felt an abiding contentment. Not because he was leaving, but because there were no cares out here. Her phone was off and there was no service. The only light was from a camp lantern hanging above the door. There was nothing to do except focus on the cake, no possibility of doing anything else until he returned, this man she had worn a dress for. Except for the cute kids at the campground and the farmers, there were no people for kilometres in any direction. She lay on the couch and breathed, fingered the ruffles on her cuffs, and let the sweet anticipation of his return consume her. In her reverie she imagined a family around her. Two boys and two girls, a dog. She imagined him sitting at the breakfast table reading and eating the breakfast she had made while she folded the clothes and then watered the herb garden.

She began washing his clothes in the sink—they would dry quickly near the fire—pounding them with a stone she took from the windowsill. She looked up from the sink out at the hidden and unknown black windows of the bush. There was a thud on the roof—a possum. She started, but the slow patter of claws on the tin reassured her.

. . .

Right where the creek met the shingle of the beach, the kids from Kongwak Indigenous Academy sat around the fire waiting for Moses, the principal, to begin the story. They had painted their faces with dabs of red and yellow.

"Sir, I'm cold."

"Nonsense. Your ancestors used to be warm with possum-skin cloaks and kangaroo fat on their skin. You'll be fine."

Moses lifted his arms up to the sky. His large belly rose with his arms and as he threw his head back his long shaggy hair flung out behind him. When he returned his arms to his side and once again faced the fire, he said:

"Listen up, boys. I promised you a story on this trip. About 1850 or so when none of this was here—no roads, no houses, no nothing—a woman went missing from Omeo or Orbost or Sale. They say she couldn't even speak English, just Scottish Gaelic."

"We speared her, eh," said one of the boys. The group laughed.

"Not funny, Elliot."

"Sorry, sir."

"Really what happened was that her husband took her little boy away from her in Sydney and came down after Angus Macmillan's men. You remember Angus Macmillan from history class. Her husband used to belt her something shocking. He was a bad man. She came looking for her little boy and ended up with our mob. Imagine them just taking in a stranger like that, feeding her from the same campfire and giving her water from the same streams, maybe even from the stream just back of here. They probably made her work a bit too. Maybe taught her how to find pippies. They took care of her and helped her get back to Sydney. And she gave birth to a little girl while she was with them."

"Shoulda chucked them all back in the sea, where they came from."

"Okay, your Mum first," said another boy.

"Nah, your dad."

The group erupted in shouting and laughter.

"Quiet, mob!" shouted Moses. "There's more to the story." The boys slowly stopped pinching and elbowing each other.

"How do you know this, sir?" one boy asked.

"I read about it in an old newspaper at the National Library in Canberra. So anyway, when the people . . ."

"You mean whitefellas?"

"Yes, when the whitefellas heard about this she was already on the way back to Sydney. But they heard about it, probably from one of the New South Wales black trackers, only they didn't hear that she'd gone back safe. So they sent out an almighty search party. They printed messages in Scottish and English; they spent months and months looking for her. And then when they still couldn't find news of her, they wanted someone to blame, so they went out with guns and massacred our tribe until there were only twenty or so left. That was just a few miles down this road at Bursting Creek."

He crossed himself and again looked to the sky. The silence was broken by a boy making gun sounds with his mouth. "Pshow, pshow, pshow! Bang, you dead whitefella!"

"Elliot, stop it! Oi! Stop it!"

The boys surreptitiously slapped and punched their neighbours around the campfire, until Moses restored order by tossing a dead ti tree trunk into the fire. The flames dashed up and smoke rushed out from under the trunk in all directions. The boys coughed and moved away from the fire circle.

"The point of the story," he went on, "is that something good—the whitefellas' loyalty to their own—led to something bad—the massacre. It also shows the importance of understanding. The whole thing could have been avoided by listening and talking."

"Sir, I heard something more about that story," another boy said.

"Yes, what's that?"

"That lady, she never left. She's still here and she turned into an owl and you can hear her screams. She's like a ghost, sir, like a banshee, remember?"

"Spirits can linger, yes," said Moses.

A silence fell among the boys as they pondered this. The breeze rippled through the ti trees, and they knocked together, making a sound like an old house at dusk.

"All right boys, time for bed. We're going to hike out to the wreck tomorrow early. Help me put this fire out."

"But sir, it's only seven-thirty."

"It's dark, the stars are out. Time doesn't matter out here, Elliot."

After some grumbling the boys all trundled off to their tents.

In the tent he was sharing with a boy called Jonas, Elliot kept flicking a lighter on and off as he lay with his back to the other boy.

"Where'd you get that lighter?"

"Stole it."

"From where?"

"Ya Mum."

"I'm gonna tell Moses."

"Nah, don't. I can't sleep. Let's go out."

"We'll get strife."

"Nah, what can he do?"

Elliot had already begun painstakingly unzipping the tent flap, holding the zipper with his right hand and his right fingers with his left hand to avoid any sudden movements.

. . .

She opened the firebox and, as she leaned over to attend to the cake, one of her pigtails slipped off her shoulder and the end landed on a hot coal. She smelled the burning keratin before she felt the heat of the flame. Then, in her panic, she reared back, slapped her body all over then ran out of the shack into the ferns and sand. A few inches of her left pigtail was gone, leaving small black chars caught in the matted and unravelled end.

She sighed deeply and lay against the sand under the ferns. She remained there for a moment. Just as she rose, she heard laughter.

Her heart pounded around her skull. She went back to the door of the shack. Again, she heard the laughter. She opened the door and called out over her shoulder.

"Scott! Is that you?"

She saw a flicker of light in the ferns and a human shape.

"Scott!"

Elliot called out, in a panic, "Who's there?"

Hearing a voice that was not Scott's, the girl ran as fast as her flowing dress would allow into the bush and away from the voice. She stumbled on a tree stump and her dress tore. She hurried away, feeling as if she would be grabbed by the hair at any moment. She dared not look back. Catching her feet on a fern frond, she slid down towards the creek bed. Her right leg nearly became stuck in a wombat hole.

The water from the creek began seeping up what was left of her dress, and she fought blindly through the twisting twigs and long fern fronds that hung over the banks, fighting the urge both to scream and be still. Following the creek, she knew, would bring her to the campsite, and there she could find help.

Elliot saw the shape stumble over a rock, heard the scream, and then the vision stood before him: a scratched, bleeding, and soaked woman in a ruin of petticoats and ruffles walking out of the bush. His only thought was to protect the others. He looked for the nearest rock that fit his palm and hurled it at the creature. Again and again, he sent rocks flying until it disappeared back up the creek. He thought he had hit it but couldn't be sure. He waited for a while, until there was no sound but the curlews crying.

In the firebox, the cake cooked all the way through, soft and moist, then, even as the fire softened to embers, it began the process of drying into a hard rock of burnt sugar, which is how Scott found it when he returned with dinner.

### The Second Vision

Mr. Headley was going into town today, so I rode with him in the dray, and he dropped me in front of Cooper's news agency on George Street. In the window I saw the headline in the *Herald* about that woman missing along the south coast in what they call Gippsland. That Scottish word they call her, the Bean. The Missing Bean, the headline said. I was in town looking for a cheap new ribbon for my hat but, even with the bustle of the city, it brought back the ferny sandy soil smell of the wombat hole I crawled down to escape the blacks on that evening. As I continued down George Street, I crossed myself. My mind went back to that journey and those long-browed dark staring people. Oh curse you, Jim Nolan, curse the day I met you.

It had been folly to leave Sydney while pregnant, but I had to find my boy. Jim told me it was going to be two weeks on a ship to Newcastle and back, a fine adventure for a young boy, but they never returned. My husband had taken him away on an expedition to the south, overland. I only knew this because a kindly army officer found me and told me. He had been with my husband's party but had returned to Sydney after some kind of dispute—he wouldn't say what—and he had found me at Mrs. Headley's. He said they would by now be at Omeo and would likely stay there through the winter. Oh, I am an impulsive woman!

I contrived to take some of my wages early from Mrs. Headley and took a rattling carriage down to Goulburn through the rain and wind. A woman travelling on her own must be cautious, but I threw my fears on the men of New South Wales, decent lots in the main, my husband excepted. It would take some type of real scoundrel to harm a woman visibly with child as I was. In my bag I had one of Mr. Headley's daggers from his collection. I returned it when I came back to Sydney. I am not a common thief, but I was desperate. I repeated the part of the prayer that goes "deliver us from evil," over and over again. "Deliver us from evil, deliver us from evil, deliver us from evil . . ."

In Goulburn I found a bullock-team travelling south as far as Bombala. The driver said for a small price he could take me the rest of the way to Omeo on horseback, for there were no direct roads. He was one of those overly talkative men but also a spontaneously protective one. I could tell it was a matter of personal respect for himself that he would let nothing happen to me. He apologised for each rut in the road and gave me his pillow to sit on. It was easy enough to pretend to be asleep to avoid having to listen to all of his talk about the philosophers and the unification of the colonies, and when I did speak, I spoke a little in Scottish to him and pretended I could not understand what he was saying because of my little English. He seemed to enjoy this as a novelty. I understood his words well enough, but why he would bother with some of his thinking I knew not. Oh, that man was a strange one to find all the way out in the bush. It was too complicated for me, and my mind was fixed so firmly on retrieving my son—I had a continuous tormenting vision of him alone in the bush, separated from his scoundrel father, crying out for me.

Oh guilt, would I had not let him go!

And everywhere we stopped the driver asked the people about my son and how to get to Omeo. There was no news—they must have gone by a different route. The cold nights we passed, and the occasional snow, which I remember from when I was a little girl walking over the heather in Scotland with my father. All the elements, and everything I remembered—my father's hands, the lonely huts in the forest—everything reminded me more acutely of my boy's condition, out alone, perhaps in this very snow.

One morning after we had reached the coast, I got up and found Mr. — still asleep, but as I shook him I found him not asleep, but deceased. The fire trace was cold, and the horse was gone. There were horse-prints leading away from our camp. I thought I should follow them, but I should not be able to catch a man on horseback. Still, I must at some point reach the part of civilisation they were going to. At great length over many logs and rocky trails, at the end of the day as the shadows were lengthened, I smelled smoke in the chilling air. I followed the smell and saw Mr. —'s hat sitting on a stump and his horse tied up to a tree and resting on the ground. The horse seemed to have no interest in me, actually to not even have heard me. I crept closer to it, tripped over a fern frond I had unwittingly held down with my other foot, and still the horse did not stir.

It was dead, as I should have seen from the beginning. No horse sits like that with its neck twisted behind the trunk. I saw the three gruesome wounds in its chest where spears had dug in deep and wide. One saddlebag was full of books, and the other held a damper that I took out.

Why would I be ashamed to cry? A woman alone in the forest like in a fairy tale. I sat down the whole day nibbling on the damper and bemoaning my fate. The baby was busy inside me, and I had no will to move from the spot.

⁂

At the first approach of the natives, I was scared and half-crawled, half-fell, feet-first down a wombat hole to escape their notice. My dress caught on the roots and billowed up about my head so I imagine I looked something like Sir Walter Raleigh, whose portrait I had seen in the newspaper, with his frills all around his grim face. I could hear the blacks stepping about near me, and I dared not wriggle down further. I suppose my breathing must have stopped.

But then I supposed that they would be rather like us, some friendly, some not, some happy, some sad. But then again, why would they be like us? They are so different after all in appearance. I really didn't know. I had seen some Aborigines hanging around the harbour drunk and angry with each other, but these were wild ones. After some soft mutterings, I heard them walk away from me, softly scraping the leaf litter and fallen sticks with their feet.

A few days later my damper ran out and my labour pains began. I could do nothing but find some soft scrub to lie in, and, insensible to all else because of the pain, I lost regard for the noise I must have been making. And when I gained my senses, there were two of them, both women as I could tell after my eyes adjusted to the dark, staring at me. They had a vicious smell, something between fish and burning hair. Then I reflected that I must not smell well myself and perhaps even worse in their estimation due to my foreign scent and the sweat of labour.

Well, it was all right after that. There was no chance of hiding. More of them came, but they did nothing at first but look. By then my labours were well advanced and the baby, a girl, came out on my blue dress that I had laid out on the soft sand and fern litter beneath me. And then how lovely came the sense of love that I remembered from my first child, enhanced by fragrance of the ti tree and the salt breeze blowing through the treetops, which seemed to welcome and bless my daughter with its sigh. I inspected her fingers and toes and the rest of her body. It was all in order and I gave thanks to Almighty

God for her safe deliverance and freedom from infirmities. And the dusky angels, as I came to think of them, all around me, made soft noises to themselves.

I felt I must do something to commemorate the birth and so with Mr. Headley's dagger, I carved a heart on the trunk of the largest gum tree, in a smooth spot with no bark. Not having named the child as yet, I could think of nothing else to add. I cut the umbilical cord by placing it on a flat rock and bringing down a sharp rock axe on it and grinding it down like a knife through a piece of meat gristle.

For the next few weeks I lived with the blacks. It was not always easy. The phrase "God help me!" was never far from my mind. Some of the older women were suspicious of me and poked and prodded me and would have done to my baby had I allowed them. Probably some superstition about a nursing mother prevented them from truly harming me. As I pounded my own clothes in the stream, I showed them how to pound the dirt and tallow out of their possum-skin cloaks with Mrs. Headley's fancy soap I had kept wrapped up in my bag. They took readily to the smell and the slipperiness.

It seemed to me as if the group of about twenty moved almost at random through the bush, but after a few days we followed a dirty brown creek to a coastline and a great wide lagoon, with white breakers beyond, sending salt mist high into the air. Dead trees stuck up from the water along the shore, and five black swans paddled across the shimmering surface. All the people of the tribe began building a great mound of sand and mud and sticks and driftwood next to the creek bed as it ran into the sand on the shingle. They seemed greatly animated, and the next evening I discovered why.

Thousands of eels came down the creek at dusk, returning to the sea. The eels were flailing and slithering through in great clumps and with a nod from one of the old men, when he had adjudged that enough had gone out to sea, the whole troop erupted in cackles and screaming and began hurling the mound of wood and mud into the stream. As the eels began to dash against the rising barrier, they were plucked out and hurled towards a shallow pit that had been dug nearby. The children began pulling on each end of an eel and flailing each other with the smaller ones, chasing their siblings and friends. It was a scene of the greatest mirth and joy and I shall never forget it. We cooked eels over the fire and feasted into the night. The taste was different to the English eel, being saltier and fishier. Oil and slime ran down our faces, and the blacks danced for joy.

* * *

In the morning they were gone. I was left alone on the shingle with the black swans and gulls picking at the remains of eel all around me and my baby. Who could blame me for crying again? I was again bereft of any help. Face the bush or walk along the beach?

I struggled through the bush, stopping to feed my baby whenever she asked. Those who have not walked this way cannot imagine how easy it is to lose oneself in the ti tree scrub, how in the gray winter the light takes on a sinister aspect and every sound of the trees creaking against each other sounds like the click of a spear or the cock of a gun.

I came to a gum forest where the trees were more spread apart. I smelled the fire before I saw the men, and as soon as I saw the familiar leather hats, I began shouting and running towards them. They were three men on horseback, surveying the district for the governor.

They asked if I had seen any blacks. I didn't want to be responsible, and so I lied. Was that bad of me? These were men of my own and probably the blacks would just cause trouble for them. Lord, forgive me. But praise God, one of them knew my husband, Jim Nolan, and had met him in Omeo. I said nothing about the unpleasantness. He said they were already back on their way to Sydney. My trip had been for nothing, but the greater news was that my son was safe, although still in his father's hands. I told everyone we met to call on me at the Headleys' of Woollahra with any news.

Being no longer pregnant, I was able to travel on horseback with the men swiftly and, after a series of handovers I arrived at Goulburn, and over the same rattling roads, at length, back to Sydney. My little baby girl seemed no worse for the natural start to her first weeks of life. The air and sun and motion seemed to be bracing for her, and while the horse trotted or cantered she slept easily in the harness one of the men kindly rigged for my back.

Mrs. Headley forgave me everything and took me back in. I snuck Mr. Headley's dagger back into his desk. My boy was found and returned to me thanks to Mrs. Headley's connections with the Governor and an advertisement in the *Bulletin*.

All through the day I thought of the Missing Bean. As I washed Mrs. Headley's linens in the sink, I remembered washing my clothes on the rocks in that stream in Gippsland.

I laid in the clean bed in my room behind the kitchen, my children asleep on the cushions on the floor. As usual, I prayed for the Headleys, my parents, and my children: and I prayed that they would find her. I who know more than all women what she must be suffering in the bush. Dear Lord, I pray for that missing woman, whose name is known to you. I pray she will be found unharmed, in Jesus's name. Amen.

### The Third Vision

A woman had gone missing from Sale. Or she had been glimpsed in the bush near Omeo. Someone had found a frill of lace in untrammelled forest. A parasol had washed up on Ninety Mile Beach. An illiterate hand on the Orbost farm had seen a flash of blond hair bolt a fence and disappear into the scrub. Or a heart had been found carved on a tree deep in unknown bush.

At this time there were fewer than twenty thousand people in Gippsland, with an unknown number of natives, and most of the good land had not yet been cleared. A rescue party of twelve men was sent out from Bairnsdale. They found nothing but a heart carved into a tree seventy leagues east into the bush. The black trackers who were with them found nothing. Along the way they dropped handkerchiefs embossed by the women of Sale with a message in English and Scottish—for there was a rumour that the woman might be a highlander—to walk away from the rising sun and to watch for the rescuers at sunrise and sunset. When the weather began to warm again a second party formed.

John Albert thought it was probably nothing. He had heard those tales of a new Somerset beyond the horizon before, in Van Diemen's Land. Prisoner's dreams. This woman sounded like that, but there was a little pay, the provisions the rescue committee provided were plentiful, and walking beat sitting in Bairnsdale with the other out-of-work lads, who anyway would still be there when he returned. Strange things sometimes turned up in the bush that the blacks had taken from shipwrecks: hammocks, writing desks, ruined barrels. Someone had even found half a sextant in the hills behind Anderson Inlet. The people of the region had put up a substantial reward for the woman's rescue.

In Sale, the head of the committee told him that he would find nothing but that a second party was needed to convince the settlers that all possible measures had been taken. "Like finding the bean in a barrel of buttons." A party of four would be less threatening to the blacks and able to cover ground more swiftly. John Albert had been through the country before with Macmillan, and he loved the tall trees and the soft ferns. They left Bairnsdale early in the morning, heading east. He was accompanied by Jim Nolan and two black trackers whom he had met in Goulburn on his trek down from Sydney: Jackie from the Monaro, and Charlie from the Tweed River. They didn't bring dogs because there was no scent to follow and dogs would make them conspicuous. He and Jim had two rifles each and they took four horses loaded with gear and food and hundreds of the handkerchiefs with the bilingual instructions for their quarry.

At first, they shot wallabies. The gunfire would scare off the blacks but would give the woman a sign that there was civilisation at hand. She might run away towards them, or the blacks might drag her deeper into the bush. Still, after a few days, when they had plenty of meat salted away, John Albert decided to stop shooting.

Each day the search party set out again at dawn. They cantered towards the rising sun between the stately trees as though through a grid of streets. Their heads turned back and forth and up and down over the tree trunks for a carved sign and towards the ground for the trace of a campfire.

After ten days they saw the heart carved into the tree. John Albert inspected the grooves to see if there was any moisture or sign of how old the heart was.

"Someone's been out here," said Jim.

The next day they came to a beach. John Albert pushed through the curtain of ti trees. At the far end of the beach were two blacks digging for sand crabs—he couldn't tell from the distance whether the blacks were male or female. He took a step and the dry sand beneath him gave way. He rode the avalanche of sand about twenty feet down and stumbled out on the flat beach. The rest of the party followed gingerly behind him. When the blacks noticed them, they stood up, gestured to each other then ran into the misty brush at the far end of the beach.

An hour later six blacks, all men, returned. They led John Albert's party back almost in the direction they had come until they arrived at a clearing with a campfire with nine men standing and one fanning the fire with a fern frond, and John Albert and his men dismounted, and Jackie and Charlie and the men spoke many things that he did not understand, and they ate bits of a blackened lizard that had been pulled out of the fire and, after many more words that John Albert did not understand, the tracker turned to him:

"They know where she is, I think, boss. I don't know this lingo well. Could be tomorrow, next week, next month. But they will bring her."

"You trust them?"

"Yes, boss."

"Tell them we'll be waiting on the beach where we saw them catching crabs."

John Albert was uneasy about these blacks. He didn't think the woman existed, so what were they bringing? What if she did exist but they wouldn't let her go and he and Jim had to take them on, just the two of them? John Albert ordered Jackie and Charlie to clear a flat section of sand just in from the brush as a campsite. The trackers then went into the shallow surf to look for crabs.

Jim Nolan was excited. "See, we're going to find her."

"And if we do?" replied John Albert. "What if she don't want to come back with us? Probably lost the ability to speak English, if she ever had it. Probably just an Irish whore."

"What are you going to do with your share of the reward?" Jim asked. "I'm going to clear a bit of land in the hills, cut down the trees and build a cabin and never let anyone bother me again."

"We'll see," said John Albert.

"Or do you think it would be enough to live on in Sydney? Start a little shop selling grog?"

"I don't know."

"Can you imagine living with them? The blacks?"

"No Jim, I can't."

"What do they do?"

"We'll never know."

"Do you think she . . ."

"An Irish whore. Who knows?"

John Albert lifted his hat off his head, replaced it, then stood up.

"When'd you come out?" Jim Nolan asked him.

"Thirty-one."

John Albert did not want to talk to Jim Nolan, he did not want to listen to Jim Nolan, and most of all he did not want to be reminded of that ship, that muster-master, and Van Diemen's Land.

"Oi Jackie, tell us one of your mad Monaro yarns. Jim, you ever heard one of these black stories?"

"No."

"Okay boss, you remember about Sheila and the bunyip trick?"

"Yes, tell Jim. It's a good one."

John slipped forward off the log he had been sitting on, stretched his legs out towards the fire, and rested his head back on the log.

They stayed there night after night, six nights altogether, waiting for the blacks to return, foraging for berries and digging for crabs, which the two guides preferred to the aging wallaby. Every day John Albert cleaned the rifles, and every day there was still sand to be found in the chamber and the action.

"What is going to happen to these blacks?" Jim Nolan asked him.

"Charlie and Jackie?"

"No, the rest of them, the savage ones."

"What do you mean?"

"You know, what is going to happen to them?"

John was about to say, *you don't even care about what happens to your own son*, but instead said: "I don't know. What do you care?"

"Oh, I don't."

"This is just a job to get on with."

The days passed in sea-spray, sun, sand, and fire. One morning, what appeared to be the whole clan this time, their furs hanging off them like bark off a stringy gum, shuffled along the beach towards John Albert's crew. At some distance the women and children stopped while the men continued towards them. He couldn't see a white face. Were they shrouding her? Had she painted herself?

The clan carried with them their totem. It was about the size and shape of a large child and dark brown. Four of them carried it high over the beach and when they reached John Albert they tried to give the statue to him, but he stepped back. The head man lifted it high over his head and brought it crashing to the sand at John Albert's feet. Its pained smile enquired of his existence. Flakes of red, pink, white, and gold still clung to the petrified torso of a woman with flowing waves of hair carved out of salt-washed mahogany: a figurehead from a lost ship.

Sand sprayed up from the impact of the figurehead and hit John Albert's boots. As Jackie and the head man spoke haltingly, but with wide smiles, John Albert laughed and thought of what he would say to the committee: "The good news is that we found her. . . . She was shipwrecked."

"There she is," he said aloud.

"Blast it, do you think they'll still give us the reward?" Jim said.

Jackie waved a handkerchief back at John. "They want to know if you have any more of these. They want all of them as the price."

John Albert unwrapped the bundle from the saddle bags and tossed it on to the sand in front of the group.

"Freshly washed by the women of Omeo. Tell them we are thankful they returned our magic, but they should never steal her again."

He brandished his rifle to make his meaning clear, and Jackie obeyed while John Albert picked up the totem and stood it upright in the sand.

"Jim, come here and kiss it." he said.

"What?"

"Kiss her. Show them what she means to us."

Jim bent forward and kissed the totem gingerly with his salt-swept lips. He wiped the sand from his mouth and spat at his feet. A murmur went through the men of the clan and there were several smiles. From the edge of the beach the women were shouting, just audible over the waves.

"She can share your swag on the way back, Jim," said John Albert. John Albert looked to the sky above the ocean; Jackie looked to the figure at their feet. They turned to each other and both grinned.

# HOW CAN WE KNOW THE WAY

Father O'Riordan knows your schedule is light, just two online woodworking classes a week and trying to avoid your housemates in the kitchen as much as possible. Sometimes you skip cooking dinner just to avoid them, eating beef jerky or mixed nuts alone in your room, and you try not to hear what goes on in their rooms. "There is no way I'm having a funeral Mass without incense if 1 can avoid it," he says on the phone. But really you suspect that he thinks attending Mass would benefit you.

You wake up that Saturday and hear the silence, really hear it, that negative buzz in your ears. Usually it would be filled with cars and babies in prams, trams, shouts, laughter, bicycle bells, windows being thrown open, the chug of the busses, but today there is nothing and you feel that a great evil has come over the world and also that the people of the city wanted this, that they think they deserved this, as a penance.

Only ten are allowed in, but Father O'Riordan isn't strict. He doesn't count you, the organist, or himself—you are fairly certain Father doesn't really care about the restrictions, but he keeps his feelings to himself—and of course there is the great cloud of witnesses in heaven present to see Madeleine off from this life. Madeleine, her name was—is—Madeleine—an old woman you saw a few times in the parish hall after church and perhaps greeted by name once or twice, and here you are swinging the thurible at her funeral while her grandchildren and friends watch from home. You had seen her sitting in the Lady Chapel a few months ago with the stillness of great agony. By then the cancer had spread to her spine.

In the choir vestry, you dress in cassock and cotter, light the coals then take your seat in the choir stall in the sanctuary, waiting for it to begin. St. Thaddeus looks down on you from his stained-glass window. Praying for the dead is one of the few things you know for sure is good and right. Lately, every other virtuous habit has seemed to have a shadow-half, an emanation or a penumbra of unpredictable character entailed in its performance. Keeping quiet, staying home, effacing yourself, all contributing to your crushing loneliness, and is it helping others, who are probably worse off, who don't have your stubbornness, your priggishness? Prayer for the dead, though, can never be compromised. "Grant eternal rest unto her, grant eternal rest unto her, grant eternal . . ."

Father O'Riordan swishes out in his black and silver vestments and welcomes the mourners: *"She came to the church relatively late in life and she was a devoted and generous member . . ."* You catch a line of the gospel: *". . . Thomas said to him, 'LORD, we don't know where you are going, so how can we know the way?'"*

No one except Father O'Riordan knows the tune of the first hymn. You have never heard it before, and you maintain your gaze toward Saint Thaddeus. The eulogies begin. The daughter clops up to the eagle lectern in her high heels and instantly chokes up. She can't get through her prepared words. Her sister joins her in support. They cry, acknowledging those beloved watching from home. Instead of being here to comfort and grieve together, it is your strange face they will see, in profile, staring straight ahead, in the right corner of the screen. Tears are contagious, but you just look at

Saint Thaddeus. Madeleine's younger brother takes over. The clichés of an ordinary life. Three kids, five grandkids, mid-life divorce. She loved her Carlton Blues Football team. Then the image of the curved back and splayed legs rises in your mind again.

There is, or was, a girl in the sauna who lies flat on her stomach and stretches her back out by propping herself up on her elbows. A sign outside says no exercising, but this probably isn't strenuous enough to count. Everything is closed now of course. Her back and legs. You closed your eyes and repeated the *Regina Caeli* in your head when she started stretching.

Trying to turn your mind to other thoughts, you remember the dream you had a week before your baptism just last year, of a hall full of people in white robes and you sitting next to Father O'Riordan and the parish assistant Cameron at the front of the billowing mass of people. A small, black, seething demon comes out of you. It is vibrating with rage and grunting as it kicks its little legs. It somewhat resembles the Magic Pudding from the children's book. Father O'Riordan turns from his preparations, softly says, in his soft English accent, completely unphased, "Oh." The demon is a simple problem to deal with, like a dropped coin from a handful of change. Father O'Riordan does something, perhaps sprinkles some holy water, perhaps makes the sign of the cross, you can't remember, and the demon shrivels and vanishes in a cloud of steam.

Eventually, your time comes. The movements with the thurible you have learned so well. Is this allowed: this transfer of thurible from thurifer to celebrant? Your fingers touch briefly and the thought flashes through the minds of all present. None of the ten bow in response to your bow and censing. You kneel and watch the ecstasy on Father O'Riordan's face as he elevates the Host. In your practiced way, you hold the thurible out to your right side to avoid inhaling too much smoke. The chain makes parentheses-shaped indents across your fingers. You begin to sweat. What will they think? No one is looking at you, it's their grandmother's funeral, for God's sake. Stop thinking about yourself. You forget to replace the thurible during the Our Father, so you have no choice but to receive on the tongue, something Father O'Riordan acknowledges with a wry smile before he says "The Body of Christ." You will joke about this with him later, at the right time. Only one of the daughters comes up to receive Communion.

With charcoal dust on your fingers, and your hands drying out from the smoke, you pick up the crucifix and walk to the front of the coffin for the final blessing and dismissal.

Only you and the organist know the responses.

"Grant eternal rest unto her, O Lord."

"And let light perpetual shine upon her."

"May she rest in peace."

"And rise in glory."

Father O'Riordan sprinkles the coffin with a sprig of rosemary as he speaks.

And then. You can't believe it. They are actually playing the Carlton Blues team song at a church funeral; a song written to celebrate the victories of a commercial sports enterprise. Don't people listen to lyrics anymore? Another thing you and Father O'Riordan will joke about. He will raise his eyebrows and tell you not to be so judgmental, while rolling his eyes. The surreality of the scene hits you again and again with recursive force. You think of the simulacrum and simulacra and laugh inwardly. Is this real? Is Madeleine or Saint Thaddeus seeing this in some way, in heaven? I'm sorry Madeleine, you say, I don't mean to laugh at your funeral.

As the Carlton song drifts out of the Church, you toll the bell as Father O'Riordan leads the hearse to the corner of the deserted main road.

Back home you change into your bathing suit in your room with the window that looks out on the neighbor's fence and the mattress on the floor. You are going to build a frame just as soon as you finish sanding and polishing the bench for the church garden. You pack your towel, goggles, and water bottle into your backpack and set out to the public pool. The sauna is just what you need to recover from the morning. Halfway there you suddenly remember why the streets are nearly empty, yet you continue on and stare through the glass doors of the baths that refuse to open and let you in.

# MATTHEW OF OURS

## 1

The children did not believe Matthew Mackillop when he told them how he had flown through the air in a great pipe with wings. They mocked him and told their parents he was a liar. "Did the wings flap like this, Matthew Mackillop?" they asked and hummed and flapped their arms while dancing around him.

"No, they didn't flap," he said.

"As if you could avoid the stars at night," some of them scoffed.

"No, the stars are too far away to worry about when you're flying," he would say.

Some of the kids envisioned a metal pipe floating just off the ground while others imagined a great spear that rose in a giant arc then landed at its destination like an arrow halted aslant in the soil. They didn't believe him, but he had, and he remembered that tired land of sand and heat, and the men that he had loved before the calamity. He was now well past his three score and ten and those times seemed as remote as light bulbs.

He lived on the mezzanine in John Dransfield's house. *I have lived too long on this earth*, Matthew thought, as his soles ached on the rungs of the ladder he climbed down every morning. Dransfield was the richest man in the village of Ours and had three wives, who each lived in their own small rooms attached to the main house.

His father had been one of the first villagers, one of those who had drained the wetlands and dammed the creek to make stable land for the people to grow their crops and build their strange houses. The villagers grew wheat and fished in the dam that Dransfield senior had made and hunted in the forest around the village for deer and wild boar. In the first years of the village, food occupied all of everyone's waking moments, but now there was a good store of potatoes and carrots laid by.

Matthew Mackillop could not work in the fields or go out with the hunting parties, so he spent his days in the attic with his quill and wild blackberry ink, writing down everything he could remember on dried animal skins: deer, boar, and lamb. For whom, he knew not. He had finished the Psalter, all four Gospels, the Acts of the Apostles, Corinthians I and II, Romans, Galatians, Genesis, bits of Isaiah and Jeremiah, the book of Job, Jonah, Esther, the important bits of Revelation, all the forms of the rosary, the low Mass and the Sung Mass, and a good many anecdotes about the Saints. He wasn't confident that all of it was unerringly verbatim, but he knew the spirit was there.

John Dransfield took a keen interest in Matthew's activity, although he had failed to learn how to read or write despite Matthew's best efforts, of which Matthew was sometimes secretly glad, for there was little vellum to spare, though he repented of this joy at another's misfortune.

He had overheard Erica, one of Dransfield's wives, complain.

"What does he do? He doesn't work. I don't like him. Can't you build a separate shelter for him?"

To which John replied, "You see how little he eats, how quiet he is. Stop your griping."

In the before times they had laughed at him, called him eccentric and weird, for his pains at memorisation. What was worse was when his parents and siblings stopped laughing and began to cast long glances at him and whisper behind his back. He was not pursuing the activities of a normal man. In truth Matthew Mackillop was the kind of man who was difficult to talk to and repelled people with his awkward intellectualism. When he was unsure of what to say to someone, he would simply walk away from them. How aware he was that he was difficult. How people at parties or after Mass always had to duck to the loo in the midst of talking to him. He was able to laugh about it; the world had bigger concerns, but still the memories stung him, although he had forgiven them all, and daily commended the old faithful at St. Faith's to the Lord.

Matthew Mackillop had wanted a large family or at least a family, but he was short and frail with a body like a cycad and the head of a termite's nest. His arms were long and dragged down his long torso. Even back then Christian women were thin on the ground, and after all they were still women. Once he had been tormented by a true she-devil, who plagued him with her hot and cold behaviour, her private endearments and her public scorn. He still heard the words of Father Michael: "Oh, you'll find a woman to make very happy someday." But it was not in God's plan.

He was old now and the people tolerated him because of that, but the truth was that without John Dransfield's protection the villagers would probably have banished him to the forest as a waste of food and water, or worse. What's more, Matthew understood this and sympathised. Life was not so easy as in his youth, so he hung back from the table and ate little, supplementing his diet with nuts and berries from the forest. "Lord, forgive them, for they know not what they do."

And Matthew Mackillop also had a secret. One day he had been walking along the bank of a creek. While lying prostrate to drink, he slipped and his head plunged under the water. In the brief moment before his reflexes pulled him out, he saw a brilliant flash of white and rainbow. Upon further investigation he saw that there was a bed of freshwater clams huddled underneath the bank, quite hidden from view. His first thought was to rush back to Ours and tell his patron about his wonderful discovery. It was a fine and easy food source that, if carefully harvested, might last in perpetuity and keep them through the lean times which were bound to come. But something held him back. Supposing the village wasted the clams, catching them all up at once in a great feast. And once the spot was known, it would be hard to keep children away or others with selfish designs. No, it would be better to wait.

He had grabbed a clam, pried it open with the sharp edge of a small fragment of slate that was sticking out of the dirt, stabbed the white flesh with a twig, and devoured it. It tasted like the abalone his father used to hunt, one of his favourite foods as a child. He carefully replaced the empty shell next to the others under the overhang.

II

The houses, or dwellings, in the village of Ours were spaced at regular intervals. This was because every house, whether a simple collection of sheets, plastic, and fabric or—like John Dransfield's—of more thought-out wood construction, was centred around a metal telephone pole. This allowed space between the houses for beds of vegetables and for chickens to roam.

The villagers believed it was great fortune for lightning to strike the pole in the middle of a house and that perhaps the right type or right combination of lightning strikes would bring all the blessings of electricity, which even the oldest among them, except Matthew, could hardly remember, back to the world. It was on this dream, a hazy time of marvels and ease, that the cult of worship in the village was centred.

When it seemed that a storm was coming, the villagers gathered at the base of the poles in their respective dwellings and recited the incantation: "Danger high voltage!"

They placed offerings of vegetables or gumnuts (which were said to resemble a crucial but lost part of the electricity apparatus) or dead mice at the base or, in the case of the more elaborate dwellings, on raised platforms lashed to the pole at eye level. At first, they used the mice brought in by cats, but Matthew had noticed Travis, the village shaman, rescuing quivering mice from a cat's mouth, which he later saw pinned through the body with a nail into the ground or the platform. Travis, in his orange and blue high-vis shirt with the word 'sparky' on the back that covered his skinny frame like a cloak, led the prayers and invocations around the pole at John Dransfield's house in every thunderstorm. The whole village gathered in the damp, dusty room to sing and pray. Only Matthew refused to participate. When the storm had passed and the villagers had left, John Dransfield would look at Matthew and sigh.

John Dransfield's grandfather and his men had rescued Matthew during the calamity. They had roamed for several months over the countryside before entering the city where they found Matthew and some metal tools and canned food. Matthew had not been told everything that happened, and he hadn't asked. In truth there were things done by John Dransfield's group that they themselves wished they hadn't had to do. But the times were tough, and Matthew prayed for all of them.

The calamity was simply the scourging of the end. God had permitted great evil so that good might come. The schools had failed many years before and churches were restricted to serving their existing members and were forbidden from proselytising, a rule that most of them seemed to accept with ashamed gratitude. They were old and tired, and the world was moving on. For Matthew, the final signal came when Father Michael told him an abortion had been broadcast live on television. God had allowed them many years even after that.

He survived the calamity through prayer, which both gave and preserved energy. When it became clear that the electricity was never coming back, he subsisted on a stash of canned tuna, having filled the bathtub and every empty vessel with water. He lay on his back on the bed counting the dimples in the ceiling, working through the prayers he had memorised.

When the men broke into the building, working their way from apartment to apartment finding useful things to retrieve, he prepared himself for the worst. They were astonished when they burst through the door to find a man alive, sitting with his back to the wall, eyes closed, murmuring to himself. As they aimed the bow and arrow at him he began reciting, "The Lord is my shepherd, I shall not want . . ." They took all his books for kindling for the campfire.

Matthew had lived not far from the village of Ours as a boy, but the site had all been marshland and he had rarely visited it, driving past on his way to school. It caused him to reflect, as he often did, on the ways of God. How this insignificant swamp of his youth should now be the lifeblood of the village and how the contours of the land stayed the same, heedless of the heapings-up of men.

## III

It was in the dark on the mezzanine—legs studiously avoiding the metal pole that rose through the house into the sky, his eyes closed, possum skin laid across the bridge of his nose and tucked into his eye sockets to keep out the smallest particle of light, like the blinders he had worn on airplanes—that the old world came back to him most vividly. In this state he could see his apartment, its refrigerator, his cupboards and drawers full of food in cardboard and plastic packages. He felt that if he reached out, he would be able to touch his computer on its desk. A computer, he laughed. Imagine describing that one to the children. They would think he was a sorcerer more powerful than Travis, if they didn't laugh even harder than when he talked about airplanes. The older folk had heard of airplanes but had never seen one. How could he explain to them that there used to be such things as screens, about the same size as a good skipping stone, that people held in their hands and could look at all the doings of the entire world. When he thought of the tortures . . .

He wondered frequently what the Arabs he had known were doing, how many of them were still alive, those bombastic, loud, hot-headed men who would quietly show up at his apartment and ask about Jesus when they were certain no one else was around. A nation of Nicodemuses. He had begun memorising Sacred Scripture to secretly proselytise in Saudi Arabia, under the guise of being an English teacher. He had thought that their conversion and redemption was going to form the bulk of his life's work, but, as usual, God had other plans. Now humanity, or at least the part of it he knew of, was reverting to older forms.

It was in the dark, trying to not hear the sounds emanating from one or other of John Dransfield's wives' rooms downstairs, that Matthew did most of his praying, for all the souls of all the dead, every name he could remember, and those he couldn't. After years of this he was down to remembering and praying for faces he had seen, a girl who had sat across from him on the train in Munich, the chefs at a restaurant in Riyadh, soccer commentators on TV. Each night more and more of these incidental faces sprung up to him, each in their unaccountable way demanding from Matthew his intercession to God. And he was happy to oblige.

IV

Because he couldn't work in the fields or hunt, Matthew spent his time when he wasn't writing trying to interest the children of the village in the contents of his mind.

One of the children, Michael, sometimes followed him on the rare occasions that Matthew left the house. If there were other children around, Michael ignored Matthew and joined in their taunts, but when they were alone, he asked him questions.

"The bread and wine you speak of, can we have it?"

"No, I cannot give you that kind of bread and wine. We need an ordained man for that."

"Can Elder Travis give it to us?"

"No, he can't. Apostolic succession must have been maintained somewhere on God's green earth, but we do not know where."

He had dreams about the Mass, dreams in which he discovered a priest in the forest. It was enough that he had memorised the prayer of spiritual communion and recited it every Sunday (or what he thought was Sunday, for he couldn't be sure), but the craving for consecrated bread and wine only intensified as he grew older. If he ever did receive the body and blood, he would probably die immediately after.

Winter was the best season for Matthew. The children had long nights with nothing to do but listen to his stories around John Dransfield's hearth-fire. Every winter they just about made it through a book of the Pentateuch or one of the Gospels. Matthew knew that in the old days a teacher would have skipped the gruesome parts of Leviticus when teaching children, but something in him rebelled against this idea. They were growing up in a more immediate world, so different from the one he had known. He remembered once long ago at evening prayer when the lectionary had directed to skip the verses of Psalm 137 about dashing infants against the rocks. Father Michael leading the prayer had gone right ahead and said the verses, with his eyes closed. All present had expected him not to, and the lines went through Matthew Mackillop like a jolt, and he shivered involuntarily. No, I will omit nothing, thought Matthew. He worried what he would do when he exhausted his store of memory.

One day he saw Erica's young daughter Kirsten face down in the middle of a circle of children, all carrying stones. Mrs. Dransfield hurried down to the circle in great alarm, but she was astonished at what she saw next. Michael had entered the circle with his arms raised as all the other children listened attentively. One by one they dropped their stones to the dust. A couple of the larger boys heaved their stones into the forest as far as they could.

V

He passed outside the village walls, which were made of bundles of small logs that had been felled when they chose the site.

These were lashed together and buried halfway in the ground, to keep bandits and needy folk out at night. He was reflecting again on how God creates Night and Day before the Sun and the Moon and why he would do such a thing. Was it that man needed coherence and natural explanation? Or that God felt it necessary to hide Himself, as it were, behind the celestial spheres? And if so, how humble of Him. Then Matthew remembered that the plants grew before the creation of rain, how a mist came up from the Earth.

He was mashing up the blackberries gently with a flat stone on a broad leaf, filtering the juice out with his hand, throwing the seed and pulp out for the birds to peck at, when Travis appeared to him.

"Matthew Mackillop, I want to have it out with you. You have been teaching the children about your Jesus so that they no longer want to make the necessary sacrifices. They come with me to the altar, but they won't kill the lizards or the wrens anymore. They just cross themselves. The hunt is in serious jeopardy."

"The Lord will provide."

At these words there grew in Travis's heart such a hatred for the old man that he vowed to destroy him. Yet his face betrayed none of this and he said, "We shall see."

When he was sure Travis had gone, Matthew went to the clam bed and ate his fill, being careful to leave plenty of stock. He hoped the guilt would not show on his face.

Before the sun had passed fully overhead on that same day, the boy Michael found Matthew reaching for a particularly well-cloistered bramble of blackberries.

He asked him about the sacrifices that the villagers made. "They say you don't participate in them. Why?"

"I know what they were built for. You didn't think they were just made so possums could get from tree to tree without touching the ground, did you? The gods that made them are not my God."

Michael said, "I think I believe in your God. I have sinned, just as you said. I lied to Erica Dransfield that we had no good potatoes left when in fact we had several. What do I do?"

"I can't do anything but baptise you. Pray to Jesus and your sins will be washed away."

Matthew took Michael down to the clam bed and baptised him in the threefold manner. But Travis had not departed from him as Matthew Mackillop had thought, but followed them and watched from behind a tree and his hatred of Matthew Mackillop grew.

VI

Quite suddenly, in a way that no one among them could explain, the potato crop in the village of Ours failed. The rot set in before they were picked, and it was beginning to affect their stores. It was as if the evil blight travelled somehow through the air. The men went out to hunt in desperation, but the game of the forest eluded them. The traps yielded three small rabbits but nothing more. When they were gone only the blackberries and carrots were left. Matthew Mackillop had to stop writing and dared not ask for anything. He remembered the bed of clams but did not go to it.

At John Dransfield's house invocations were made constantly. Travis made offerings of pinecone and gumnut all day, slept on the floor at night, and rose early to begin the prayers again. Some of the men began to discuss leaving the village to find food. They said, "We should go now while we still have energy." They wiped down their knives and brandished their spears. Some even whispered that Matthew had a pile of animal skins in his bedroom that could still be crisped over the fire and eaten.

That very night John Dransfield called the whole village under his roof to listen to Matthew. He felt it would take their minds off their troubles. The same children that mocked him gathered attentively under the watchful eyes of their parents.

He began to chant in the Middle Eastern style that was his own innovation. He drew out the words in semi-tones and deeply plunging melodies:

"And Jesus said, A certain man had two sons: And the younger of them said to his father, Father, give me the portion of goods that is mine inheritance. And so he divided unto them his living . . ."

As he continued singing, although he had his eyes closed, he noticed a change come over the people in the room. An aura of peace and attentiveness surrounded his frail voice. Matthew looked around the circle and saw captivated eyes. He stopped singing at the point where he always began to forget the story.

"Yes, yes, what happened next?" said John Dransfield, his eyes glinting in the candlelight.

"It will come back to me."

The hush in the room intensified then slowly began to fade as a child squirmed. Just then the words returned.

"But when he was yet a great way off, his father saw him and had compassion, and ran and fell on his neck, and kissed him."

When he had finished, the room broke into applause, and several women were crying.

After the village had left to return to their homes, Travis, who had kept vigil at the shrine in John Dransfield's house for several days, asked to see Matthew alone outside.

"I know you know the secret. I was only a child then. You are a powerful man. We need your help."

Matthew replied. "I tell you truly, I do not know how to help."

"I heard the stories from my grandfather, how you could keep a house ablaze with light all night, make ice in the height of summer, talk to someone on the other side of the world. If we do not honour the gods, they will not bless us with these gifts. You, you wicked man, you remember. You know their secrets, and you work your magic against us. Think of what you are keeping from us. All our people are labouring under heavy burdens that could be made light. The drudgery of the women of Ours, the burdens on the children. I heard that a child in the old days wasn't required to work at all. Women had water and a cooking fire in their houses whenever they needed them."

Matthew Mackillop said nothing.

"You survived! No one alive is within fifty years of you! The gods must have favoured you!" Travis was shouting now.

"I have never denied that your forces and spirits are real. They are simply less powerful. In fact, they are fully enslaved to the majesty of Christ Jesus who allows them, out of love and hope for their redemption, some scope to operate freely in our world. There is nothing to fear from them."

"How did you survive?"

"I just refused, that was all."

"Refused what? What do you mean?"

"God saw me through. I say to you, Travis, I will pray for deliverance from this famine to my Christian God, and you ask your forces or spirits."

Travis gazed up at the nearest telephone pole and said, "May your presence awake and bless us with your bounty. Glow anew, glow anew, glow anew. Danger high voltage, danger high voltage, danger high voltage."

Matthew closed his eyes briefly, then said, "It is finished. We will see who has the true God."

The next morning Matthew found Michael and said, "Michael, raise a cry and say that you have found the clam bed. Then lead us to it. Say that God, our God, led you to it."

There was great excitement as Michael roused the village with his shouts. The villagers were amazed at the bounty. Michael sank to his knees in front of Matthew Mackillop and gave him thanks, saying that Matthew's God had led him through the forest with a ball of light that had settled over the clam bed.

The villagers ate of the clams. Even Travis ate a clam, but then he said, "It is not a miracle, I saw these two out here eating many months ago. He has sent the boy there to pretend that his God has delivered us."

But the villagers knelt and with loud voices gave thanks to Matthew's God Jesus.

And Travis could not abide this insult. It was false, he knew it was false. He knew that only blood could end the famine. To prove it he rushed home to fetch his spear and run it through Matthew Mackillop. Travis knelt at the pole in the centre of his house and threw his arms around it. When he returned, he drove his spear with all his considerable might into Matthew Mackillop who, with his last breaths, made the sign of the cross over himself and Travis. As Matthew fell over into the babbling water, the boy Michael saw the angels whisk him away to Paradise, and many of the children of Ours grew up with the same memory.

# HEAT NUMBERS

After practice on that first Friday of the season, I lined up in front of Coach Kelly with the rest of the Parkview Piranhas to have my heat numbers for Saturday's meet written on the inside of my forearm in felt-tip marker. It was my first season in the nine-and-ten age group. Girls had odd numbers, boys had even, single digits for the medley relays, teens for butterfly, twenties for backstroke, thirties for the individual medley, forties breaststroke, fifties free, and sixties for the free-style relay. The numbers were an organisational convenience for the adults, who didn't want to delay proceedings on behalf of a child's forgetfulness. As the meet progressed, the upcoming heat numbers, black on white plastic, were rotated on top of a big pole near the starting blocks. I suppose it was one way of teaching self-reliance. Although I was among the fastest in backstroke (the hardest stroke because you couldn't see in front of you and had to use the flags to time your flip-turn), I was one of the slower girl nines-and-tens. My numbers the year before had usually been twenty-three, thirty-three, and fifty-three. If Kirsten Runstrom, my arch-rival in backstroke, was sick or on vacation, I also swam plain three, the backstroke leg of the medley relay.

That day I went home with my friend David Hermenescu. Actually, his mom was more a friend of my mom. They had met as part of a babysitting co-op that formed in our neighbourhood when we were little. David and I maintained civility and played together as a silent acknowledgement of our mothers' intimacy, though he often smelled like fertiliser and recounted to me episodes of cartoons I'd never heard of and didn't care about. It was David's first year as a Piranha and his first Friday of numbers. He got three races: fourteen, twenty-four, and forty-four.

We lived a few doors away in a double-story tract house identical on the outside to the Hermenescu's, but their interior was marvelously superior to ours. They had wood flooring where we had cracked tiles; their fridge was stainless steel with a place that dispensed water like the soda machine at Carl's Jr; they had decorative columns in the dining room, indoor plants, and a grand piano with wheels, where our electric Casio had forty-four keys; their backyard was lined with slate and had a small fish pond, where we had a loose brick path leading to our back gate; they had granite countertops, where we had laminate; their front door had frosted glass hexagons set at eye level, where the green paint on ours was peeling off; air purifiers and humidifiers ran in most of their rooms, where our house most often smelled like Zipper, our Pekingese cross. But it was their staircase that impressed me the most: floral wrought iron supports with a polished wood banister and spiral newel.

That Friday, I was drawing a picture of apples in a bowl at the kitchen table while David fed their newly hatched chicks in their incubator. I had just learned from Mom the technique of filling in large spaces with colour by rubbing pencil shavings across the paper with my fingers, and I was busy with the golden bowl while simultaneously admiring the large red five on my arm that I had been given because Kirsten had chicken pox and couldn't race.

Shadows on the wall loomed as David adjusted the heat lamp. David's father Luke (short for Lucretiu) came in and drew a glass of water from the outside of the fridge. He gave me a small wave with his free hand but then, setting down his full glass, he strode over to the incubator and yanked David's arm until David was lifted clear off the ground.

"What's this for? Who did this!" Luke barked. The chicks squeaked in their incubator.

"They're my numbers for tomorrow."

"Wash them now. Don't let anyone do this to you ever again. I don't want you getting poisoned from the ink, okay?"

Of course, mine had to go too. I wrote the numbers down on my drawing paper. We scrubbed the numbers off with soap, but they'd already started to stretch out into our skin. I could still see the faded shape of mine no matter how much soap I used. Luke brought us two thick rubber bands from his upstairs office and we copied the numbers down onto them with a fine-tip pen. Then we rolled them onto our arms.

When I went home, I told Mom the numbers were poisonous. "Reina, they aren't. I wouldn't let them give you something poisonous." I didn't quite believe her. I knew Luke was a scientist. When we went on family trips out to the desert, he showed us planets through his telescope. I saw that Mars really was red and that Saturn had rings. He had started a company that developed software for the designing of microscope and telescope lenses.

The next morning at the swim meet, I informed my friends that the ink on their arms would probably kill them before the first race, by lunch time at the latest, for sure.

"Why would they give them to us, then?"

"They just don't know."

"Well, why don't you tell them?"

"I'll get David's dad to tell them."

A big older boy said: "Are you stupid? I had numbers written on my arm last year and I'm still alive."

This was hard to refute, but Luke was the smartest person I knew, so I thought it would be best to have him tell the coaches. He was easy to find at the pool. His top half was big like a bottle of milk, but his legs were skinny and pale below his khaki shorts. He wore a yellow polo shirt tucked into his shorts and strapped sandals with long blue socks. When David swam, Luke cheered and stood with a towel at the end of his lane, but he did not want to be there. He wanted to be with his computer programs and his microscopes.

"Mr. Hermenescu, can you tell Coach Kelly that the markers are poisonous?" I asked.

"Sure, I'll tell her."

"Thanks."

David and I wore those rubber bands around our arms all season. I always wondered how the other kids survived ink poisoning. Even though they and my mother had challenged it, the belief in ink poisoning stayed with me, even if it didn't immediately kill you, and I took great care with my pens and markers at school.

In those days I knew of only one house grander than the Hermenescus' and that was Luke's father's house high up on the cliffs in Pelican Hill, overlooking the ocean. I accompanied David up there one rainy night, "to see the house," Mum said. From the garage we took an elevator into the kitchen and from there stepped into the revolving living room. At the press of a button, you could go from looking out the double-glazed windows at the sea and the cliffs to watching the news on TV or watching your guests come down the hallway. I imagined old Mr. Hermenescu getting fed up with the television and violently holding down his button to view a more soothing scene. It was raining heavily that night, and there was nothing to see as I pressed my nose into the hematite window.

Leading into the living room there ran a large hallway done up in what I later knew to be the style of a Roman atrium with frescoes, thin Doric columns, and a fountain surrounded by variegated *laurentii.* Along the right wall stood a full bookcase with a false mid-section that, if pushed, led to a room with metal walls: the fallout bunker. It had a large circular lock like a bank vault's. Later I would realize it had been built exactly like a bank vault. Rows of canned food and bottles of water rested on shelves beside a small generator, a portable electric stove, and a bed that folded down out of the wall.

The old man was asleep upstairs, so David and I ate pasta cooked by his third wife and watched cartoons on TV. When old man Hermenescu died, Luke inherited the mansion. They sold it for five and a half million. David's mother called around the neighbourhood to give the figure. "They just sold his monument to America," my mom said as she hung up the phone.

For a long time, Luke and the numbers were a great mystery. It wasn't until history class a few years later that the outlines of the Hermenescus' story snapped into place. Grainy footage. An arm. Numbers.

But until then I knew that adults were the key to this and other childhood puzzles. I was notorious for listening to the adults talk, lurking on staircase landings, behind doorways, under tables, and on balconies, but I wasn't sure what to listen for. The New Year's Eve party was at the Hermenescus' house that year of the numbers. David and I avoided the other children stuffed away with their Game Boys and foosball in the garage. We crawled up the stairs and I lay prone on the landing the entire evening next to him, looking through the filigreed railing, breathing through my mouth to avoid his smell, watching the adults talk and laugh and attend each other. Along with the thrill of something more to learn came the idea that I was too young, that I was not yet suited to knowing, which I felt then as a great injustice.

# RENDER UNTO

Nathan isn't wearing a mask. It's Tuesday morning Mass, the first after four months of shutdown, and I have just looked up from reading the welcome. There they all are, fifteen or so—surely the largest weekday congregation in the diocese, just saying—all with the toothpaste blue or a more tasteful solid black or flower pattern on their faces. Face-nappies, as SkyNews called them last night. I have to remember to see the dignity behind them. These are the regulars and it's heartening for me to see them still showing up. All there except for Madeleine, who is in hospice dying—from cancer, not the virus. I must remember her son Orlando at the intercessions. He is locked in his room at the care facility and unable to understand why.

During the Alleluia the voices are muffled, except mine and Nathan's. I've just started using a French medieval chant in a minor key that seems to fit the times. When he came up for communion, I tried to keep my face neutral, and even gave a slight smile. Just two more years until retirement.

When the churches were closed, I was proud of the fact that I never locked the door. It was always open, slightly ajar, and I knew people had come in because I saw them, or their little artifacts: pen caps, chewing gum wrappers, prayer requests, or the traces one can't avoid—footprints on wet days, a kneeler not replaced. I knew the place so well I could tell at a glance when a pew cushion had been sat on. During the shutdown—I prefer that word to lockdown—we had Mass every day, just Nathan and I in the house. Our associate priest Father Matthew came once a week, which was all his scruples would allow as he lived in the flat behind the church, and so technically belonged to a separate household. While the lockdown had just ended, the eight p.m. curfew was still enforced, as was the five-kilometer personal restriction "radius" (except for emergencies), and various bewildering and inconsistent number caps were placed on every form of human gathering. It was fifty in a church, one hundred in a brothel, two hundred in a pub—something like that.

I wish they would scrap the five kilometre thing. Last week one of the old ladies, Marjorie, came to the door in tears—they were rolling underneath her mask and off her chin—saying that she had gone half a kilometre outside her radius. She was convinced the cops would find her by the signal from her car's navigation system.

"Should I turn myself in, Father?" she said. Well, I put her mind to rest and sent her on her way.

. . .

"What can we do about Orlando?" asks Cath, my parish treasurer, helping herself to coffee in my kitchen as is usual after weekday Mass.

"Nothing right now. We're not allowed to visit."

She is silent for a while, then says, "Surely there's something that can be done?"

"Nope, no visits, nothing."

"On compassionate grounds?"

"I wish. They've just had an outbreak, so they're still on total lockdown."

Nathan makes scrambled eggs as usual, and I have toast. Of course, I say nothing to him during breakfast in front of Cath and Father Matthew. I had learned it was usually better to address troublesome things after a period of time had passed. I would prefer to wait a few days, but there is Mass tomorrow morning, so I will have to address it tonight.

As we do every Tuesday, Cath and I discuss the finances—which at present are almost embarrassingly healthy, so we have little to discuss, a great blessing. We are so familiar with each other that several conversations go on over the weeks without the need to explain. Which is why she can say, without preamble, "I don't mind if he wears a mask or not, but think of Rosemary and Elizabeth. They're almost ninety."

"I'll speak to him tonight."

"Luke twenty, twenty-five."

"Yes, I know. He's my parishioner. He's my friend. I have to do what's best for his soul."

"Yes, we all love him. If only he knew."

When she leaves, I glance at my computer. There's an official complaint from a parishioner who will remain nameless about Nathan and his face with the archbishop's office cc'ed. Already? Sometimes, honestly, these people. I reply that I will be handling the matter and will be in touch if I require any assistance.

There he is, out there in the driveway with the Persian man. We ran a food bank during shutdown out of the rectory garage, but now the Persian man is the only one who comes. And he comes every day. Mask around his chin. I tried to tell him to come once a week, but he has nearly no English comprehension, poor man. And yet he bangs incessantly on the door and won't leave. "Ah, nothing," he says, putting his hand in his mouth.

"Wednesday! You are to come every Wednesday, no more!" I told him yesterday.

"Ah, nothing," he said, pointing in his mouth.

But it's clearly not true. His belly protrudes from under the purple YMCA t-shirt I've never seen him without. He is grateful, it has to be said. He kisses the cross around his neck as he's leaving and says, "Brother, brother. Thank you, brother." That's our nickname for him: Brother, Brother. Patience, patience and prayer. Why can't the poor ever be reasonable, I ask the Lord sometimes. Brother, Brother would take the whole garage if you weren't there with him. We keep our nativity decorations on the same shelves as the tins, and he tried to stuff the little dark-skinned doll we use as baby Jesus into his cart full of food. He points at the cans and packets of napkins, saying, "Ah, her? Ah, her? Her? Her?" Her, meaning "that one?" He must know by this point that there are no others.

I see the Persian man kiss his necklace and wave goodbye to Nathan, who comes back in the house and heads upstairs. Like clockwork he will come down in ten minutes with a book and go sit in the park with his coffee, even now when the cold brings a mist that makes the day seem like it never starts. I don't know what he does the rest of the day. He was doing some online teaching in English and giving a couple of our kids piano lessons in the church hall, but all of that stopped and now he mostly lives off an inheritance from his mother. No one knows how large, or how small, I suppose, it is. He pays me rent and board in cash every month.

I have to give Madeleine last rites today, which is tricky because it's the only reason a visitor is allowed. I want to time it right to stay in the good graces of the hospital. But of course, I can't leave it too late either. I've been waiting for a phone call from the daughter, who is semi-estranged. Complex, as most families are. I calculate how long I should wait before calling her.

As I hear Nathan leave for his reading, I breathe out slowly. There was something I remembered reading—in Newman, I think it was—about what the Anglo-Catholic churches had done during an epidemic in the nineteenth century. I spend the next hour in my study flipping through my books, which helps me forget the world outside and even why I was reading in the first place.

I put my mask on to enter the hospital. I sign in, pretend to pump sanitiser on my hands, rub them together. Three nurses are chatting in the corner with their masks around their chins. As I walk past, they pull them up.

Madeleine's mask has fallen down below her nose. As I enter, I see the attempt at a smile in her eyes. She looks smaller, as the dying often do. On the table next to the bed is a photo of her and Orlando and her two daughters, when the children were little, framed in ceramic white roses.

"Father Lawrence," which is not my name, she mumbles.

"How are you, Madeleine?" But the answer is obvious. It's good I came today. She is in and out, drugged and dazed. I watch her for a while, holding her hand and praying silently for the relief of her pain and a good defense before the judgement seat. I take my mask off. What does it matter? I feel imprisoned: watched and judged. I unpack my case with the materials for last rites. Anointing her forehead with the sign of the Cross, I realise it's been so long since I have touched anyone.

"Father Lawrence, I think I want to drop out of school," she says.

"That sounds good."

"I'm so glad you agree. My parents don't understand."

. . .

During the first shutdown, in the absence of anything to do in the evenings, I started playing chess online with my glass of wine and clips of the hymns at World Youth Day 1999. I love the part when a—what are we meant to call them now?—developmentally challenged boy gets up on stage and JPII waves away security and embraces him and listens as he speaks in his ear. Makes me cry every time.

I used a picture of Saint Mary Mackillop as my avatar, as they say. It's amazing how God arranges things such that anything to which you pay close attention can teach you about the world. I thought I could tell when a male player was trying too hard not to get beaten by what he assumed was a woman. I played ten-minute, no-increment games, long enough that you weren't rushed but short enough to be fully engaged. I started noticing patterns in the nationalities. Russians and Serbians played very slowly, deliberately. They were easy to defeat on time. Indians played fast and brought their queens out early, often much too early. Americans usually tried to gimmick you. If you knew the gimmick, you could win easily.

Chess is a funny game. Become too fixated on one attack and you lose on the other side of the board. Bunker down and fail to attack, and you'll get opened up eventually. It's a game of finesse and intuition, proportional action, windfall, and psychology. A year after I started my account, I got an email from the chess website about my stats. I was astonished to find I had played more than a thousand games during the shutdown. My rating hardly budged. I had almost an equal number of wins and losses, with a few draws.

. . .

He comes in after curfew—the government's, not mine, as if I would ever be so gauche as a landlord—and after I've had a few glasses of wine.

"What's this about not wearing a mask? It's the law. I know how you feel, but you have to do it," I say.

"It's not so much that I won't, it's that I can't," he replies.

"Oh, come on." This is teenage stuff. "I'm not saying it's not absurd."

"The absurdity is the point."

"They're doing their best. It's a hard time."

"They're not even trying. It's a fake problem. The mask is a sign of submission to a lie."

His voice is growing louder.

"This isn't a war," I say. "This is not the hill to die on."

"Then what is?"

I ignore this.

"Believe what you want, just put it on."

"No. It's a sign of fear. Christians shouldn't be afraid of death."

"It's the law."

"It's an insane law."

"I'm a priest, a responsible person. A public person. I can't go openly defying."

"Oh, yes, the precious reputation of the church. Yeah. I think people would respect the church more if they did break the law."

"I can't have politics in the church."

"It's not political, it's metaphysical."

"But everyone else will see it as political."

"That's not my problem."

"But it's mine. The Lord says we are to render unto Caesar, meaning obey the earthly authorities, even if we don't wish to."

"Is this made in the image of Caesar?" He points at his face.

"That's not the point."

"Then what is? You can't tell me that covering your face during Mass has no meaning, Father. No spiritual meaning, I mean."

"Maybe it does, maybe it doesn't."

"I emailed the archbishop about it when it was announced last week. I said that given that in restaurants you don't have to wear a mask and that Mass is a communal meal we shouldn't have to either. You know what he said."

I can guess. "No," I say.

"He said, or one of his minions said, that there was a requirement to put your mask back on between bites. Can you believe that? It's a lie."

That is what I expected. I can't respond. I can't agree that the archbishop is a liar, and I can't defend that absurdity. But then again, Mass is more than a communal meal.

"Yes, I agree there are inconsistencies in the government's response, but they're doing their best."

Nathan rolls his eyes and does that irritating raised-eyebrow, closed-mouth smile. I love him, but he can be a right git.

"I couldn't even hear anyone during the Alleluia, except myself. Do you think it's honouring God covering your face like that?"

Here I draw up and stand with righteousness.

"Are you saying those people today weren't honouring God?" I ask with force in my voice.

"Well, no, but."

"You have a certain arrogance sometimes."

"You were the one who taught me to follow the truth."

"It's a very serious matter, and very foolish to deny yourself the Sacraments."

"I'm fasting, like everyone else was during lockdown. And," he adds, "it might be a mistake, but you have to let me do it."

He storms off upstairs, and we don't speak about it again. I can feel the anger coming off him at dinner every night, no matter how outwardly polite he is. It's almost like watching a toddler having a breath-holding tantrum. The parents are worried but also admire the resolve. The way to torment him the most is to ignore his anguish, so I do.

It remains in the back of my mind, and it arises whenever I see him—which is relatively frequently, as we live in the same house— but I trust God will put it all right. I find myself spontaneously rehearsing new retorts to him from our argument while I am in the shower, or otherwise unoccupied, which is not often. We pray for him every night at evening prayer.

It is all the more painful because I know he gets it. I remember clearly, it must have been some weeks after he started coming to Mass, and my focus happened to light on him as I held up the host and said, "Behold, the Lamb of God." I saw his eyes open, as if following my instructions, and knew that he was there for the same reason I was there, the same reason I had become a priest. Amidst all the people who were there for their parents or their children, or their spouse, or their friends, or for the organ music, he and I—and to be fair our church had many like us—were there for the same reason: to have our lives redeemed by the only Redeemer.

Nathan's baptism was such an encouragement to the church. A few months later one of his friends was baptised. They both invited friends who merely dabbled, but the age profile of the church shifted downward. It was wonderful to see them both growing in devotion, learning about the faith. Nathan learned to serve at the altar and, when his housemate overdosed, I invited him to move in with me. How many priests in the diocese could say they had altar servers in their late twenties? He was one of the first successes we had, and not the last. I hope I am not disorderedly proud in the growth of the church. There were fifteen at my installation three years ago; now we get that on a regular weekday. On Sundays we are full, perhaps eighty to one hundred, and on Easter and Christmas before the shutdown even the side chapel filled, and the latecomers had to stand at the back.

I was his confessor for a few months, but when he moved in, I felt it was better if he stopped confessing to me. People think that hearing confessions will make you dislike people because you hear about them at their worst, but it's actually the opposite. The intimacy that I have developed with penitents far exceeds those who never or rarely confess. The priest is just the conduit of Christ's grace anyway. All I can say is that his sins were nothing on mine: scarlet, magenta, fiery flagrant sins, the deliberate misuse of myself and others. But dwelling on your sins gives them power they don't deserve. God calls some men to be priests not because they have unique gifts, or not only because of that, but because He knows there is no other way they will fight the good fight.

Weeks go by. Slowly life returns to the city. More people emerge to stroll the streets. The pub across the road roars back to life, and I realise I had become accustomed to silence on weekend nights just as I was accustomed to sleeping through the pounding noise of the pub, called "The Refuge," before the shutdown.

We are cordial in the house, but I can feel his pain. It is painful for me. I miss him at Mass and prayer. But life goes on. Rosemary enters hospice care. The refugee family the church supports is being evicted from their apartment by a Chinese landlord because they haven't passed on information about a rent increase to the parish council and so are quite in arrears. One of the homeless men who comes for a free lunch on Wednesdays strokes the hair of the teenage daughter of one of my parishioners who had just started helping prepare the food. I have to ban him from staying. He can pick up his meal, but he can't stay. The ebbs and flows of life. My niece has a baby, but we aren't allowed to visit, my sister's rules.

I find what I was looking for. It isn't in Newman. I am showing Cath a picture of the Church in Sussex where I was ordained and the book, *Churches of North-Western South-East England*, or something like that, falls open to a black-and-white picture of a plaque in an Anglican church in Maidstone that says, "It was during the typhoid epidemic of 1896 that the daily offering of the Eucharist was begun in this parish." Well.

A fox gets into the garden, and I interview a potential new curate, Daniel. I like to have active interviews. It keeps them away from their prepared answers. So, he and I pick both of the backyard olive trees clean. I pretend it just has to be done that day. It is a good activity, actually. He is up the ladder with the tennis racket, battering the top branches. He'll make a good priest if he can keep his head out of the theological books.

Nathan skulks around the house. I have to remind myself often not to resent him, but it is hard. "You have to let me." He is right. I, and the vast majority of the country, could think he is foolish and cutting his nose to spite his face, but he is entitled to do so. You can't force people to church anymore, though ironically, Nathan might be one of the only people who would consider that a good idea. "I would be happy if you were King of Australia," he told me once. As one does, I learn through the grapevine that he has begun calling our Lord's Supper "Masquerade Mass." Less than two years now to retirement.

. . .

Madeleine dies and we have the funeral. Only ten are allowed, so it has to be filmed. I would have asked Nathan to do the incense and the reading, but knowing his commitments, that was a nonstarter, so I called another young man I knew, who had been too much alone of late. I only feel sorry I couldn't do as much for others; because of the outbreak at Orlando's home he wasn't allowed at his own mother's funeral. At breakfast the morning of the funeral I want to tell Nathan about Orlando, which of course he knows, being part of the parish, but I want to rub his nose in it like parents tell their kids about starving children in Africa when they won't eat. But a deep breath, a *Lord Give Me Strength*, and I go back to some story in the paper about China buying up the Philippines.

. . .

At evening Mass for the thirtieth anniversary of my ordination, he is there in the middle of a pew, maskless. A couple of the other young men have them around their chins. It is a glorious service: Bishop David preached a wonderful sermon, and afterward we have champagne and fancy canapes in the church hall. Cath organised a mashup of congratulatory videos from my friends in England, Africa, and around the world. My dear friend, who is a Swedish bishop, says "I wish you many more decades in ministry," but with his accent "decades" sounded like "dickheads." I see Nathan and his friends giggling rather indiscreetly, sitting with their backs to the grand piano. Cath asks him to play some light music in the background after the video, while people are mingling and eating and drinking. "Wichita Lineman," "What a Wonderful World," tunes of that sort.

When I come by to talk, he says: "It's us, we're the dickheads. I wish you many more dickheads."

Because there is food and drink, no one wears a mask. He starts playing "My Way" because he knows it would irritate me. I had once preached against the playing of "My Way" at Christian funerals. It should be called "His Way," I said, or something cheesy like that, pointing at the crucifix behind me.

Then I put my wine glass down, boot him off the stool, and start playing "I Will Sing the Wondrous Story." All the young people gather around the piano. Nathan sings loudly with his rough and ready voice, in tune. When it is over, he puts his arm around my shoulder and I do the same to him. We stand that way for maybe a minute, taking sips of wine, looking out at the ladies who are clearing the tables and stacking up the chairs. Some of them have their masks back on. Well, it's best not to dwell.

In the morning there is an email, which I skim. "no mask . . . formal complaint . . . jeopardising the safety . . . refer you to public health advice . . ."

Oh, what is this life? The endless complaining. In the end it's just you and God, you and Christ, and you and the Spirit, Who's always in front of your nose. I don't open the email from the Arch when it arrives. It's from some aide, no doubt; he wouldn't even be aware of the complaint. One-and-a-bit years until retirement.

And then the rules change, and Nathan comes back to Mass. I visit my new grandniece, but it is never the way it was. Nathan gets married—I perform the ceremony—and moves out of the city. The whole thing lasts a widow's mite of the interdict against King John. I don't think I would have been pleased, in the end, if he had worn a mask.

# SPARE US YET

*Judge of the nations, spare us yet*
*Lest we forget, lest we forget.*
—Rudyard Kipling

Cameron and his mother Miriam arrived in the early evening, just before the heavy rain, after four hours driving along the dirt roads in their rental hatchback as children ran in and out of the roadside sugar cane, as the brahmin cattle tied up at the front of scattered shacks watched on.

The hotel was an old colonial house with a full wrap-around wrought-iron balcony and mature palm trees covering the roof, like umbrellas around a pool. It had the kind of decayed air that would attract the eye of a high-school photography student working in sepia. There was a view of the north-side beach from the front verandah and as he waited for his mother to slowly trudge up the steps, the afternoon light and the shallow beach took Cameron back to a childhood memory. His friend Austin Rogers pulling a leopard shark into their inflatable kayak, the high sheen of sun on water and the cliffs, the smell of sunscreen, the unnatural colours of the snorkels and fins around them, the greens and pinks. The cliffs and the rising island sprinkled with red toyon. The lifting, no, the scooping of the shark into the kayak and Austin's smile under his blonde bowl cut as the creature thrashed its way back over the walls and into the swarm of its fellows.

Miriam had just finished a round of chemotherapy and was paying for the trip, and despite his frustrations with her she was good cover for what Cameron considered to be his real purpose. The country had recently come under the rule of its military commander. Elected representatives had been frog-marched out of parliament at gunpoint. A senior minister, the son of a long-dead statesman, had fled by boat to a neighbouring nation and begun denouncing the military authorities. The papers were full of outrage. Had there been a violation of sovereignty? Would the two nations begin hostilities? Canberra and Wellington condemned the new government. The military commander responded by expelling foreign correspondents and ambassadors. Cameron already had two pitches to write about what was going on accepted by Australian magazines. As far as he knew, there were no Western journalists left in the country. He had published two long articles on Australian colonial bush literature in a quarterly magazine, but his name was otherwise unknown. If he could pull off some true investigative reporting, it might make his name back home.

The hotel was on the north side of Viti Levu, where few tourists went; most of the action was at the resorts on the south coast, closer to the international airport. At the other places they had stayed, the staff had been impressed that they were travelling together. "Many young boys don't enjoy travelling with their mother," the waitresses would say, flashing smiles. Cameron never knew what to say to this. Did he enjoy it? He was by nature timid and travelling with his mother gave him a built-in excuse to avoid the partying that went on in the evenings and well into the nights. Most of the young people he had met on the trip had irritated him somewhat. There was the Queensland girl who told him she came to the island to get away from the cold weather, and the English pair on the sightseeing boat who insisted they weren't a couple, just good friends. The woman—a South London Indian, as it happened—had started speaking to his mother, and their laughter resounded over the whine of the engine as they took in the island chain at sunset. There were the boorish Queenslanders watching State of Origin Rugby and drinking the same beer they would have had at home out of yard glasses, in the same weather. "Come on Maroons!"

His mother would get a little annoyed if he came back to the room too early. He knew she was worried about his sociability, particularly with girls. "You're not shy with girls, are you?" she asked one day.

"It's ok, Mum," he had said.

His favourite part of the trip so far had been hiking to an abandoned stone village at the top of a small island off Beqa Island. Cameron remembered looking back down the trail from the peak, looking down on what his guides were explaining had originally been a corridor of attack and defense: a bowling alley for defensive boulders, hot water, and flung stones. But what a costly strategy. He imagined the exhilaration of waiting for the right moment when the attackers were near, the pressure on those hiding and releasing the boulder, that poised moment, the glory of a hit, the bodies strewn along the trail and pressed against the cliff-face, the tragedy of a miss, the irretrievable boulder scampering down to the sea. And he knew he was capable of tough deeds. When he had returned after the hike, the lodge owner had said that an Israeli soldier had broken his leg on the same trail six months earlier.

After they dropped their bags in their upstairs room, Cameron and Miriam went to the bar and ordered gin and tonics. The barman was apologetic about a lack of ice but said he would send someone out for it and their drinks would be ready in fifteen minutes. There were only two other people in the bar, an enormous native man and his female companion, both about forty years old, with several empty bottles of beer and two nearly full ones on their round wooden table, the only place one could drink aside from the actual bar, which had only two red leather-topped stools. They both smiled at Cameron and Miriam and beckoned them to sit down with them. As Cameron stood still, unsure how to respond, the bartender came over and told Cameron and Miriam that dinner was ready for them in the dining room. Cameron smiled and held up his hand to the pair.

There were more than twenty white-clothed tables in the dining room, all empty except for the table next to the one the bartender led them to, which was occupied by two older white men, the first they had seen since leaving the capital. They all ate in silence until the fruit salad came for dessert, when Cameron couldn't help himself. In an outburst that was more curiosity than conviviality, he said:

"That looks tasty."

"Oh yes, of course," replied one of the men.

"What brings you both here?"

"Healing in a shed by the rugby pitch. It used to be a big, tall building, but it burned down. But Jesus doesn't need fancy buildings. I was a hunchback for ten years, but Jesus healed me. It was nothing I did. It was all him, and he's been doing it here. People who couldn't see, people who couldn't walk, all healed by him." The man looked up, as if suddenly unaware of their presence. He hit his hand on the table.

"Buddha and Allah and Muhammad: all those people are dead in the ground but Jesus rose. He said if you have faith the size of a grain of mustard you can see mountains lifted off the ground."

He paused to take a sip of Coke.

"And, so, uh, what would you recommend we see around here?" Cameron asked.

"There's nothing better than seeing people healed."

Cameron mumbled assent, imagining that he sensed scorn from the men for the frivolous holiday-maker they took him to be. He thought of the exhibit they had seen in the capital museum about a missionary who was killed and eaten in the nineteenth century. The village had had bad luck ever since and had eventually invited the descendants of the Reverend back for a ceremony to ask their forgiveness. There was a photo of the hundred or so villagers with a cluster of white faces in the middle, along with the sole of the Reverend's left shoe, complete with teeth marks. These men, these supposed healers, it dawned on Cameron, were pansies, pikers: not like the Reverend from the museum. They didn't have to worry about being eaten. If only they knew his real purpose here: unmasking the regime from within. The trouble was there didn't seem to be anything particularly wrong with the country. Nothing that Cameron could see on the surface, anyway.

◦ ◦ ◦

In the capital his ambitions had been frustrated. A contact in Melbourne had put him in touch with a Chinese businessman who had been a classmate of the military commander at the Marist school. Mr. Bai was in the early stages of developing a resort, the first one of its kind on the North Coast, to try to attract more tourists to the region. It was this that gave Cameron the idea to go there. When they met, Mr. Bai, a gray-haired, late-middle-aged man with a garish electric blue Hawaiian shirt covering his tall frame, had requested he leave his voice recorder behind. Mr. Bai said the regime had protected his business and was strongly supportive of the tourism industry. He said only that the commander had been an average rugby player at school, "but much better than me, of course," with a laugh. In the end they spent most of the time talking about what would happen if a tsunami came to the coast. "Very bad for business." And then Mr. Bai had had to go to a fundraiser for the local Chinese school. He did not invite Cameron.

He read the papers every day, but that could tell him nothing. He had tried to meet locals without divulging his purpose, but his efforts had been met with variations of rejection ranging from humoring a madman to evading a creep. He would start off by asking a waiter or a stallholder to assess his Fijian pronunciation, with its cees that sound like dees and qs that sound like gees. When they were sufficiently baffled, he would ask about the government and get mostly laughs over the shoulder.

He watched videos, including one where the military commander took an Australian journalist with him grocery shopping—this was from months before, before the journalists were all kicked out. He was picking up milk and lettuce, chatting to the cashier, just like any normal person. An old woman began complaining to him about the sea wall erosion near her village, and he had given her his personal phone number and promised to take care of it.

At around four o'clock every day the rain came in. While his mother rested upstairs, Cameron ate his late lunch on the lodge deck. On the used book table in the lobby, he had discovered a tiny hardback copy of Kipling's *Barrack-Room Ballads.* The Kipling book was more or less the only thing worthwhile. There were a bunch of second-rate Australian novels, fitness guides, marriage counselling books, and a Soviet edition of Gogol's *Dead Souls.* Eating his chicken curry on the dining balcony, he read the Kipling through quite quickly. He was the only patron of the restaurant, and he thought probably they were the only guests at the hotel. The five waitresses doted on him, and he savoured the irony. None of the waitresses would have any idea who Kipling was. Kipling: so unforgivable yet so captivating. When he came to the end of "Recessional," the last poem in the book, he set the book down and looked out over the little lagoon. Hundreds of pale iridescent tilapia swarmed below his hand as he set his elbow to rest on the rail. He picked a few grains of rice from his plate and tossed them into the water. A foment of fish tore at the food. Implode, and not explode, was the word his contact in Melbourne had used: "Any day now, that government is going to implode."

"You're a better man than I am, Gunga-din," said the waitress when she cleared his table.

And then finally one of the trade union contacts he had emailed before he left replied with the email address of a local activist, Shastra, a young Hindu woman. She agreed to meet Cameron at a coffee shop at the only mall in the city. In the air-conditioned glass Starbucks knock-off, she told him about the regime's rule: how women were tortured at the Naval barracks, how the newspapers were prevented from criticising the government. These were the juicy details his prospective editors would love, if he could get her on the record. Shastra invited him to a talk on the new constitution that was being given that night by an Australian legal academic. The talk would be held in the conference room at the Holiday Inn. All the people he needed to meet and speak to, many of whom had been escorted out of Parliament at gunpoint, would be there.

The academic lectured on the procedures by which a new Constitution could be drafted, using East Timor and several South American countries as examples. Cameron had once sat in on one of her lectures at Melbourne University, even though he was not enrolled in the class, because a girl he was friendly with had raved about her.

When the last slide of her PowerPoint, a picture of brown hands raised towards the camera, had changed to a blank screen, she took questions. From what Cameron could tell, there were no questions about the legal processes, only denunciations. "How can we trust these same people who were willing to use violence?" "What they do at the barracks they must be punished for!" "Why won't Australia and New Zealand boycott the rugby tour? You are all talk!"

The question and answer concluded, and Cameron went to the back of the room to the refreshment table. As he walked between the empty chairs, he recognised a man from the photos he had seen in the newspaper: the military commander's right-hand man, a short Indian lawyer with a severe face, said to be the mastermind behind the coup. He was sitting in the back row in between two bodyguards, who wore green fishing vests, pockets bulging with pepper spray and other security paraphernalia. He had listened to the whole of the proceedings and shook hands with and politely greeted some of the men who moments before had been denouncing his government, as they too approached the back for hot coffee, fruit, and tiny sandwiches. Cameron saw one of the bodyguards dip a triangular tuna sandwich in his mug of hot coffee and swallow it in one bite.

Shastra was standing with a small group around the academic who had spoken. Cameron took his tea and plate of fruit and stood next to her. He was introduced to the circle but withdrew before any questions could come his way. He set his nearly full mug of tea and plate down beside the hot water dispenser, left the hotel, and took a taxi back to the lodge.

* * *

The native man and woman were still sitting at the table in the bar when Miriam and Cameron returned. A young boy arrived carrying a bag of ice over his shoulder, which he heaved up onto the bar.

"Your drinks coming now," said the bartender.

"Where you from?" the man asked, beckoning Miriam and Cameron to take the empty chairs at the table.

"Australia," Cameron said as they sat. The bar had a concrete floor and all whitewashed walls and no décor except for an enormous Carlsberg sign. It was like a mean English pub except the doors were propped open to try to catch any sign of breeze off the ocean.

"Oh yeah? I been to Australia, Rockhampton. Rocky."

"What were you doing there?"

"I'm a rugby coach, there was a rugby carnival there."

Miriam introduced herself and her son. The man's name was Jonah and the woman's name was Mariwalesi. The bartender put their iced drinks down on the table and watched as the faith-healers climbed the stairs to the upper rooms.

"Jesus this, Jesus that. How was your dinner?" asked Jonah.

"Great, thanks. Haha, yes."

"We spoke to them two nights ago. Fakers."

"How do you know?"

"Ah, they all are, tricking poor people. I am a Christian, so I know." He held up his beer bottle. "They are like Muslims, those men, they don't like beer. I like beer."

"You are—iTaukei?" Cameron asked, using the native word for themselves.

"Yes, you know that word?"

"I did some research before we came."

"And you are Mary Wallace," he said to Mariwalesi.

"How do you know that? You must read books a lot."

"Too much," Miriam said.

Mary Wallace, as Cameron had read, was a famous wife of an early missionary, who was so loved that the local version of her name, Mariwalesi, had become a popular girls' name.

Cameron was itching to ask the two of them directly what they thought of the current government, but he did not want to risk putting them in trouble.

"Yes, I drink too much, but I am Christian. Like you."

"Oh really? No, I'm not Christian."

"You are Christian, all white men are Christian."

"We've been to the museum. You weren't always Christian, your people I mean."

"No."

"Neither were mine. So, what happened to all your ancestors?"

"They were saved when the chiefs accepted Christ. Instantly."

"What happens when, if, you all stop believing?"

"The ancestors who believed will be ashamed of them, but they will be saved by the ancestors."

Cameron and Jonah exchanged a look of astonishment, a mutual embarrassment at the swift candour. They both laughed.

"Now, we drink."

The four clinked their glasses.

"And Madam, are you enjoying our country?" Mariwalesi asked.

"Oh yes, it's wonderful, so beautiful and everyone so friendly."

"Young men don't often enjoy travelling with their mothers."

"Haha, no, they don't. But we're doing all right, aren't we Cameron?"

"Yes, Mum."

"When Mum shuts up," Miriam said.

"Yes."

Cameron put his arm around her. I have been too harsh with her, he thought. He wanted to show the love he bore for her. He often resolved to do this when she was not around, but when the woman was there in front of him he could not let his feelings translate into action. He gave her blank expressions, short answers, and exasperated sighs. Why can't I treat her well? She wants to know about me because she loves me.

"You know a lot of them didn't change so much," Jonah said. "Me, I want the old ways back. All of them. Including the old thing we used to eat . . . I mean beef."

"I think I will go upstairs now," Miriam said.

"I'll take you up," said Cameron.

"No, you stay."

He watched her frailty take the stairs.

Jonah spoke: "Back in the old days, when one of us became a Christian, he had to go and kill his old spirit animal. A symbol that you rejected the old ways. My grandfather, his spirit animal was the tiger shark so when the missionaries came, he had to go kill one.

Those guys were crazy back then. No mask or scuba or anything. They took half a goat out with them on the boat, and he dove down holding his breath, with weights around his waist. He took the half goat down and tied it to a rock and waited for the tiger sharks to come. Every few minutes he would come up to breathe then go down again. That damn shark never come. Lots of others, nurse, whitetip, blacktip, thresher, all came but never a tiger shark. The spirit animal, he knew what was going on."

"So, what happened?" He imagined himself killing that shark underwater with just a diving knife.

"The priest and my grandfather prayed for the tiger shark to come, and he went out every day with the same routine. But soon they were not able to spare any more goats, so he just went to the spot and dove and dove. Still the shark doesn't come. So what does my grandfather do? He tells the village and the whole island that if someone catches a tiger shark it is meant for him to kill."

"So did he become Christian?"

"Not if he couldn't kill one shark. He washed up on the beach with suction marks all along his back. He was held down by that octopus, who didn't want him getting her shark. We have an old story about a shark god who is defeated by an octopus. It's a story about man and woman: the man is the hunter, the shark; the woman is the octopus who will drag him down with her smothering arms if he doesn't watch himself."

Cameron grew bold. "Yes, we were out on Beqa Island, and I went on a hike up to the top of one of the small islands there. There was an old village made of stone up there and the guide said that the people used to live at the very top of their islands for defense, because all the islands were fighting each other, and they would land in canoes and attack each other and throw down hot water and rocks and spears on the attackers. And then when the missionaries came, there was peace and all the villagers moved to the beach where it was easier to fish and grow food."

"Maybe yes."

"I'm not Christian, but maybe you have to say there was some good there."

"Maybe yes."

Jonah continued: "We are the same, you and I. There is a book. Maybe I shouldn't say the name. *Melanesian Aryans.*"

"I don't know about that."

"They said that there was no way such a fine-looking people could be anything other than Aryan."

"The things people used to believe."

The bartender came and took their glasses away and replaced them with beer for Jonah and a gin and tonic for Cameron.

Cameron sensed his moment.

"What about the Commander? What do you think of him?"

"Who?"

"The president."

"The president is the president. There's always another one coming."

"But, you know, is he good for the country?"

"What about action? We are just talking here," Jonah said, as if he had not heard the question.

"What should we do?" Cameron asked. The two drinks had put him in a fatalistic mood. He felt that he wouldn't care if he ended up in jail. At least that would be something to write about. And then he remembered his mother upstairs, probably reading some horrendous memoir about growing up in Africa or something. Mariwalesi, too, had drifted upstairs at some point not long before. Cameron now became aware of her absence.

"A cow. One of the Hindu cows. Let's take one."

"What for?"

"As our spirit animal. I'll hold it down. You take a knife from the dining room and cut the throat. We have steak."

"I don't think that's a good idea."

"They are vegetarian. They can't hurt us."

Cameron tried to laugh away the horrifying idea.

"It is your spirit animal," said Jonah.

Seeing the horrified look on Cameron's face, he laughed and said, "It was fantastic to meet yourself and your mother; we should go to bed now. Good night."

. . .

When Cameron opened the door, his mother was grinning.

"Great news, I just got an email from Doctor Glass. I'm in remission."

"That's wonderful!"

She read from the screen: "No visible signs of malignant cells! They don't know for sure yet, but the first test looked great."

"So we won't need to go down to the shed tomorrow."

"No way!" She laughed. "What do you make of all this spiritual stuff, Cam?"

"I don't know, Mum. I think it's hard for us to understand. The spirit world is very real to them."

"You know everyone was baptised except me. By the time I came along Mum didn't care. She did the first five. It was just what you did back then."

"I know."

"Are you getting some good stories?" she asked after a while.

"No one seems to want to say anything."

# FAREWELL TO THE WELL-KNOWN OLD BAILEY

*"Farewell to Old England forever,*
*Farewell to my rum culls as well,*
*Farewell to the well-known Old Bailey,*
*Where I used for to cut such a swell."*
　　　　　　—*"Botany Bay" (convict song)*

*"I said in my haste, every man is a liar."*
　　　　　　—Psalm 116:11

You have no real plans in London. The savings you built up from processing documents for the Department of Education in Melbourne would last, barring unexpected needs, another six months at least. There is no urgency to do anything. You wake up with no alarm then wander to one of three or four coffee shops in the local area. If the weather is pleasant, you read in a nearby park on a wooden Barcalounger, glancing up from Aristophanes or Mishima to watch the idle and crazed of Swiss Cottage pass by.

You get to know the staff at your favourite café. They are French and extremely pleasant, not like what you have heard about French people. One of the girls there, Jacqui, takes a liking to you. You do long sets of push-ups and sit-ups on the floor to Bach's harpsichord concertos and Australian hip-hop. Concerto in D Minor followed by Jimmy Recard. This is the life you had dreamed of, the break you needed. An unknown man in a new land with no demands and no limits.

After a week with a private room, the backpacker's manager asks if you are willing to move into a dorm because a couple wants to book the private room. You agree and meet two Canadian girls who are staying in the dorm, one white, one black, both a little dull but eager for experience. Together you wander around Hampstead, moving in and out of bars, people-watching, guessing about the relationships of drinkers at nearby tables. You teach them to walk on the footpath without giving way. Simply look above and beyond the person walking towards you; they will get out of your way. The white one is amazed and has a grin like you have given her a new power. She would sleep with you, but they are a pair, and the shared room makes it impossible.

On Friday night you lie in your bunk and stare at the ceiling. You listen to the noise from the corridor where the international girls and boys are drinking. And the worst part is that your complaints are also an old cliché, the malaise of youth, treated by a thousand authors. While most will understand you, none will truly sympathise. You feel your entrapment so acutely, while others, like those outside your door at this very moment, are content to descend into the glow of drunkenness.

The black girl comes into the room to get her coat.

"Hey!" she says brightly, smiling at you. "Do you want some vodka? We're all drinking in the corridor."

"Yeah, give me a minute," you say.

You take a deep breath, finish your reverie, and join the others in the corridor.

With the two Canadians there is a Serbian and a Guyanese man and a Spanish couple, all drinking from a bottle of Nikita Imperial.

You nod around to the group and say to the Guyanese man, who is closest to you: "My brother, I'm black like you."

He thinks you might be mocking him, so he is unsure what to say. You enjoy doing this.

"Um, what?" he says, which you are used to.

"I'm black. Aboriginal Australian."

"Wait, really?"

"Yes."

You take a swig from the bottle.

"Yep, coming back to recolonise England."

"Wow, it must be so interesting for you to be here," says the Spanish girl.

The Serbian looks at you. You can tell what he's thinking: "But you don't look Aboriginal." Of course he won't say it. Say it, fucker.

. . .

It starts with a thought experiment. Because you were in London, you were reading *The Secret Agent* by Joseph Conrad, a novel set in London when the anarchist menace was gripping Europe. The anarchists in the book are deciding what their next target of attack should be. They reason painstakingly through their various options. Not a politician or a monarch, at the risk of creating a martyr. Not an indiscriminate attack at a train station, at the risk of bad press. Not a famous or beloved building, at the risk of same. Finally, they decide to strike at the very heart of what the bourgeoisie believe to be the foundation of their prosperity and stability—namely Reason itself. How to attack Reason, Science, Progress, and Comfort? Blow up its most powerful symbol, the place that orders and demarcates the precise hours and minutes of the bourgeois life of getting and keeping—the Greenwich Observatory.

It sets you thinking, via memories of photographs in school textbooks of Buddhist monks incinerating themselves, what would be the equivalent of this today, or rather, where is a potent symbolic place for a similar attack? Or for a self-sacrifice? Promptly eliminating such obvious, clichéd, and mundane targets as mosques, schools, and public streets, you ponder this question. Parliament would be much too difficult and not likely, in this age of credulity, to have the desired impact. No, you decide, it must be self-sacrifice only and great care must be taken to ensure no collateral damage.

But where? There are iconic sites in Australia herself. Uluru? Too sacred, and your act is likely to be misinterpreted as for the sake of Aborigines only. Sydney Opera House was too modern; Port Arthur already had its grim modern-day moment; Fremantle Gaol, good but too obscure; Norfolk Island, too out of the way. It needed to be a place where the meaning would make instant sense, wake up the people, make them see as they read the news, go to the window, and think, my goodness how has it come to this? The War Memorial in Canberra was not a bad choice. But you are in London. There are resonant totems here of course.

When you visit Westminster, where the whole scheme, the whole Botany Bay debacle was cooked up, you want to scream, "You fuckers, you faggots!" but you just mumble the words under your breath. The impudence of the place that has no idea of your feelings, no knowledge of the apocalypse breathed forth from these stones on the underside of the planet.

They usually shut right up when you say you are Aboriginal. Sometimes you even show them the picture of your great-grandfather, a full-blood man from the country around Cloncurry. But some part of you always feels dirty, like you were using your ancestors, deploying them strategically in a false game of holiness that had nothing to do with you. Would your great-grandfather, who fought off troopers and pastoralists for weeks with his tribe of brothers, appreciate that you invoked his memory to quiet a drunk woman at a party before taking another dexy and eventually passing out with a half-rolled cigarette in your hand on the bed of an equally unknown woman whom you barely remember taking ketamine with in the toilets?

You have a type of contempt for most aboriginal activists. Their position is fundamentally founded on weakness. All this nonsense about black bodies, systems of oppression, stolen land. You want to say to them, *Bro, just be your own system of oppression.* You want to say, *Do you think our great-great-grandfathers would understand or have any respect for you and what you are saying?* They would already have finished the raid and would be resting by the fire with a fat kangaroo tail, or be with the spirits, having died with honour.

"What, bro?" you remember saying to one of them. "Are you gonna ship your own mother back to England? Really?"

It must be said that the white activists are worse. The condemnation of their ancestors was the final and greatest insult of the coloniser. Men who condemn their ancestors can't be trusted.

Your country, Australia, a property market with a government, an ignorant sex-obsessed people. You have a profound love and a profound hate for them. They are your people, but they have no people. They are profoundly silly, you think, with no struggles, no fire, no grit, no manhood, no seriousness, no ability to say no. Your fellow Australians, the men especially, would never know what it was like to hunt a snub-nosed *Procoptodon*, or head into the unknown interior, or land at Gallipoli. As a famous author you read put it, "they have put us out to pasture."

And yet, as you lie in your bunk listening to the rain and your roommates in the corridor screeching and passing yet another bottle of vodka between them, you have to acknowledge that you yourself have never approached the feats of your ancestors either, but at least you are self-aware.

Your Aboriginal friends argue that the white man took it all away, and your white friends can't see that it is all being taken away from them. They are like orphans who are told every morning that tomorrow is the day a happy family will gather them up. The family never comes, but the promise is repeated. New Albion, the Workingman's Paradise, the land of the fair go is over. All that's left is the choice of which bar, which coffee shop, which city, which girl, the choice of which feed bowl for an animal in a zoo. Meanwhile, the suburbs crowd with more and more foreigners who know nothing of your ways beyond your government processes. You tell your white friends that they need to be careful with their country.

At university you remember a seminar on finding your purpose in life. It was a mandatory introductory module in the final year. There was a fat middle-aged woman teaching. She introduced herself and said the program of the day was used frequently by her in large business settings. The first exercise was a worksheet calling you to fill in your primary values.

The first student to share his primary values with the class was a small man with wispy red hair. "I guess I thought about it for a while," he said, "and I guess my supreme value is compassion."

This answer made you want to vomit. He looked weak. The trouble was that compassion was his only option. He couldn't choose a different value even if he wanted to. Could he tell you on what metaphysical basis, from what cosmic vista, he holds up compassion?

You went to the toilet and never went back to the class. In the mirror you looked at your reasonable muscles, flat stomach, and springy legs. Not an Arrernte warrior from Baldwin Spencer's book, but not bad. You could accept defeat at the hands of a superior enemy—but from this colonising faggot who was not half the man his ancestors were, whose prime motivation is "compassion"?

At least the memory of that pathetic face gives you renewed motivation while swinging the kettlebells in your room, but is it really his fault? He's as much a victim as anyone. And you regret your anger, and yet.

There is a story that you read in high school which has always stuck with you. It is about a hanging in Hobart in the early days. Twelve men are to be hung, but the hangman is too drunk to work and the condemning magistrate has no taste for the job, and to solve his dilemma he attempts to recruit one of the twelve to hang the others in exchange for a pardon. The magistrate goes down the line asking each man in turn if he wants his freedom. They all refuse. He offers not only a pardon but the permanent billet of executioner. They all refuse. One says, "What would my old man think, me turning straight like that? I couldn't live with myself."

The magistrate comes to the final and the youngest of the group, who agrees to his terms, who is indeed ecstatic to be condemning the rest. I hope I would have the guts to die with the rest, you think.

* * *

Sitting in the park one morning you attempt to write:

*This collapse is different. It resides in not being able to go beyond platitudes with your countrymen. It involves not sharing your deepest fears with your family. The collapse is in mandatory lies. It is in perpetual hedging and hope borne of fear, not of love. The collapse has no fire or physical destruction, yet. It is in seeing people for use, as one-dimensional people. An inability to be serious about serious things, which leads to despair, social death, failure to reproduce ...*

*What I want is no less than the best for everyone. I want everyone to thrive in their own ways, reach their potential, in accordance with nature, and not only every individual but every nation. And how is this to be done? We must be permitted to find ourselves again.*

*This I propose to call re-racinated. What does it mean to be re-racinated? A relationship with your heritage ...*

*And the colonisers, what about them? They are us, we are them now ... Like a great Australian poet says, they brought the end of the world and the rest of the world.*

*Modern Aborigines are culturally one part Aboriginal, one part cockney, one part Irish and one part Black American ...*

*I am convinced that the Australian inferiority complex is misguided. Our deep wells are here, if they can be seen. Britain contains us. Beowulf is mine. But we were Britain's castoffs. As castoffs we felt inferior. But the blood is renewed under sun and hardship ...*

*Last night I had a dream of Father Lyndon, fat old Father Lyndon, with an aggressive manner I never saw in real life, interrogating me, pulling me out of a coffin propped up on two sawhorses in the nave of St. Faith's, accusing: "Why did you do this? Think of your soul!" But why? Surely God would understand, if it was for a cause, and not for a selfish reason. Surely recklessness in battle is not the same as suicide. The three hundred Spartans knew that they would die if they remained. Was that contemptible in God's eyes? We Australians are in a battle, but so few are fighting. What obligations do I have? A samurai committing seppuku after dishonour is not the same as a modern suicide of despair.*

*I am a man like my ancestors, with a clear vision, a place on earth, an obligation to do my best for my people . . .*

*Remember the transportees, the convicts, the sufferings that built our country . . . For hidden Australia, for aristocratic Australia, for White Australia, Creole Australia . . .*

They are good thoughts, you think, but all false starts. The impulse to write quickly dies. Who would listen or be capable of understanding? Where would you publish? You are again alone with your thoughts.

* * *

You move back into a private room at the backpacker's as the winter holidays end. As you idle more and more in London the idea of going back to work becomes more and more distasteful. But your money is running out. Life became too comfortable. It was like your job with the state government. You could get away with wearing sneakers and jeans every day because you knew no one would say anything. You took long smoke breaks and waited days to reply to emails because you could get away with it. You grew to have contempt for your supervisors and colleagues. Idling took more out of you than you thought it would. In London there is no one to keep up appearances with, no one to care. Without meaning to, you stop washing your clothes and showering. You have an extra coffee instead of doing sit-ups in the morning.

One morning in the communal shower, as you turn your face into the stream, your plan quickly crystalises with great clarity, a sparkling vision. The Old Bailey: the place from where so many convicts had been sent. The place where the people who had dispossessed your ancestors had themselves been dispossessed of their liberty. At this stage it is a fantasy, elaborate like an erotic fantasy with certain images repeated over and over again: the two flags, Aboriginal and Eureka, a great rush of people in a city street, soldiers marching, Circular Quay in dazzling sunshine . . .

Everything about it must be carefully crafted and enriched with symbolism. The date the day the First Fleet left England, the very hour, if you can find out what it was.

The 26th of January, as appropriate as it seems, would be misinterpreted to dishonour the Aboriginal side of your heritage, and it's only a few days away. You need more time.

You aren't sad or despairing, there is just a gray, dead feeling; a feeling that nothing would ever interest you again; no one new would enter your life, every type of person had passed through your gaze. But there was a pleasure you felt, a pleasure best experienced in company, the pleasure of a secret. The larger the group the more exquisite the relish of concealment, the pleasure of future significance, the knowledge that these people would know your name and think back on this moment, remember your eyes and your movements, and try to wriggle into your thoughts.

* * *

Yet, amidst the deeper feeling of inner death you are suddenly happy in your purpose. You stop smoking. You study drawings and plans long before you buy the planks. Jacqui from the French café calls you and wants to see you again.

"You're so mysterious," she says.

As you walk with her around Hampstead Heath, scarves heaving in the early spring wind, you want to tell her what you are planning.

"I'm going away, Jacqui," you say.

"Yes, we are all going away," she says.

"No, I'm really going away."

"I will come visit you wherever you are."

"Thanks, but you can't."

You get an email from your aunt. Your mother has died in Cloncurry. The drinking finally got to her. You have no money for airfare and the date of the plan is only two weeks away. Now there is no one to disappoint with your death. As torn as you are, this seems like a sign you are on the right path. You don't reply to your aunt's email or another one she sends a few days later. You stare at the photograph of your great-grandfather that you always carry with you. You stare at his dark skin and at your own light hand, wondering where he is inside you. Let it be resolved in the next world.

You can't think of your mother, but a memory of your cousins slaughtering a stolen sheep in your bedroom in Cloncurry when you were a child comes back to you. The smell of the blood, the way they had rousted you out of bed and shoved the furniture against the wall to clear space. It was a world you had to leave.

You fail at building the scaffolding. It would be much too cumbersome anyway to transport, and to build it there would give too much time for interference. But it must be a hanging. Anything else would so easily be misinterpreted. You scout out the building and are shocked to find that the Gothic courthouse in your mind has been replaced with a steel and blue-glass high-rise. There is a sturdy lamppost at the front of the building. It will have to do. You order the flags online.

All the comings and goings of city life. The desiccation of life, the fundamental unreality of this tiled floor, these papered walls, the space beyond your nose outside the blanket that you pull over your head to think. Life is as good as death. When you complete the act there will be no difference. But then how will a deliberate death have meaning? How can it resound in your fellow countrymen if there is no difference?

You gather the world in your hand like a glass Christmas tree ornament in a box. The city of London looks like phone chargers and thumb drives.

* * *

It is May 13th, the day the First Fleet cleared the heads of Portsmouth Harbour in 1787. The news comes in late to the Sydney wire. It is a small item that gets your name wrong and is pushed out of the news cycle once determined to be a suicide:

"An Australian man was found dead in London at the site of the original Old Bailey. The man, identified only as David, was found wrapped in Eureka and Aboriginal flags . . ."

Again you drop, dangle, writhe, no going back, and then, again you wake in the top bunk, shouting: "God help me!"

# LYNBROOK

That day, the train tracks buckled at eleven, so it was lucky that I was at Heidelberg station by seven and on the bus to Inverloch by five to eight. Already it was thirty-six degrees. As we left the city the bus driver called out the stops and noted down which ones the passengers needed, in order to avoid those they did not and speed up the trip. "Anyone for The Gurdies? Corinella turn-off, Grantville . . ." Inverloch was the terminus, so I did not need to call out. There were few passengers that day, and we all knew why.

My aunt had called me the day before to ask if I was free to check in on my grandparents and stay the night with them. It was going to be hot. They were not managing well.

"They cover for each other. Hide their memory loss. As long as they're together nothing will change," she said.

They had no air-conditioning, none of that terribly wasteful expense. "Terribubble," she would say in her child's voice, "a terribubble waste." This also applied to central heating, sparkling water, washing the car and, most frustratingly, showers. When I was a teenager and she felt I was taking too long in her shower she would turn on the taps in the kitchen, making my water alternate between cold and hot until I couldn't stand it any longer.

The bus did have air-conditioning, but I only had to press my hand against the window to feel the heat outside. There was no livestock in the jaundiced fields and the trees shook in the north wind.

When I stepped off the bus at the bottom of the main street the temperature had increased from the morning and, as I would later learn, it was nearly halfway to the boiling point. I became soaked in sweat more or less instantly. A hint of char in the raging air. Patches of moisture spread on my shirt where the straps of my backpack dug in. And then, disconcertingly, I was no longer covered in sweat. It had all dried up. It hurt to open my eyes and I kept them half-closed in a blizzard squint.

On my visits to town, I usually got a pie and chocolate milk from the good pie shop—the one that used a picture of my grandfather licking his plate on their brochure—but there was no question of that today. It was near the water, fifty yards out of my way. The main street of Inverloch rises steadily from the waterfront to the hill that my grandparents' street was on. I walked halfway up the slope and entered the bad pie shop like a polar explorer entering a sauna. With my cheese and bacon pie and bottle of water, I stepped out again into the oven. The north wind whipped into my face. When it's cold we speak of a wind-chill factor; well, this was a wind-heat factor. The great gusts of hot air blowing out of the desert centre of the continent. I understood what wilderness survivors in the snow, whose tales I had devoured in my grandparents' lounge room, meant when they said the cold was such that all they could do was exist. Existence was an effort, let alone walking, but walk I did, past the Japanese restaurant and the Vet, and the mini-golf course opposite them that had so enthralled me as a child, past the senior's club, and the fire station. The trucks were gone. I remembered one plane-crash survivor in Canada I read about who trudged miles and miles through the snow with a broken left ankle, telling himself that if he broke the syncopated rhythm of his footfall for even a moment, he would surely die. Below the wind I heard my own footfall and my own breath harmonising in a rhythm of their own. As I climbed the hill, the rhythm slowed. To stop is to die, I told myself. Having finished the water bottle I just bought, I shook the dregs out and the drops evaporated before they could appear against the grey bitumen of the road.

. . .

The house was in darkness when my grandmother opened the door. I knew she was trying to keep the cool of the night trapped, but it was a losing battle. She was wearing a loose blouse and shorts and I realised I had never seen her bare legs before. They were riddled with purple veins. She offered me an ice pack from the freezer and wrapped another in a tea towel to give to her husband. The pulsating pom-poms of the gum leaves from the trees they refused to cut down sounded like rain on the corrugated iron roof in the hot wind. I checked the thermometer that hung from a nail in the side of the bookshelf. Ninety-six degrees in the old style.

The house smelled of that familiar smell that I always associate with visits to the country. I think it was a blend of all the old books— school presentation copies of Hamlet, Robert Browning, Shelley, Dante that had been given to my great-grandfather around the turn of the previous century—mixed with the daily pot of porridge and the unvarnished wooden floorboards. It was a sweet, not unpleasant, foresty, sandy-soil smell, amplified by the heat, with a hint of rotting carrot peel from the compost tub next to the kitchen sink.

We went down the long corridor and opened the door that divided the front half of the house from the back. This door had a rubber strip along its bottom designed to keep the warm air in the front half of the house during winter. On a day like this it had no use.

My grandfather was in the back room sitting in a chair in the middle of three heroically whirring fans. He was leaning back in a low chair with his head thrown back over the chair and a towel that I assume was once cold across his forehead. He looked up to greet me and said something, but I couldn't hear over the old black leatherbound radio blaring an emergency broadcast. The whole state was on fire. Temperature records broken everywhere. Forty-five degrees in Melbourne and it wasn't even afternoon. The announcer urged people to evacuate as soon as possible if they were in an area of danger or be fully prepared to stay and protect their property. Have your essential documents and valuables in the car ready to go. If you don't leave as soon as the warning is given it may be too late. Moreover, nearly all city transit was cancelled. This is where I learned that the train tracks I had been on a few hours earlier had buckled.

I leaned in to shake my grandfather's hand.

"Bloody hot," he said.

"It sure is."

"Here, darling, here's another ice pack," my grandma said, placing the tea towel-wrapped item on his thigh.

I told her I was going to Tasmania in the mid-semester break and she told me to say hello to Wattie for her. Wattie, short for Walter, was her grandfather who died in 1935. My aunt had warned me about this, that her mind slipped in and out of time without showing it, but it was still a shock to see it in person.

"Oh, I will," I promised.

She sat down at the upright piano and began to play a Bach minuet.

"Stop that, we need to listen," my grandfather bellowed.

I remembered the funny names Grandma and I gave each other. We had different names but on any given day we were always the same—me Rork 1, her Rork 2—or whichever name we had for the day. I remember playing behind the cushions, her pretending I was a lump hurting her back. I remembered the Olympic games we held on the back verandah with some classmates from school and how Ernie, the old man from next door, whose house Gabe bought, won the 100-metre dash across the verandah in his electric gopher scooter and how he said it was the thrill of his life. I remembered dodging and flicking away the bull-ants while climbing the tree in the front yard. All while my mother had her treatments in the city. This was where I first suspected the non-existence of Santa Claus when I saw the Gameboy box on the high shelf in the back of the closet where I had gone to hide from her behind the stacks of *Overlands* and *Australian Geographics.* How we would drive out to bushland singing "Botany Bay," "What Can the Matter Be?" "Aura Lee," and other songs, how at night on the way back she would turn the brights on and off for oncoming cars like a deeper rhythm under our singing, and sometimes a wombat or roo would appear in the scrub before scurrying away; how if it was a fox or a rabbit she would swerve (within reason) to kill it.

* * *

The voice on the radio: "Evacuation orders in effect for Seaford, Lysterfield, Lynbrook, Upwey . . ."

"Get in the car!" My grandfather bellowed, leaning his head forward like a baby trying to sit up. "Let's go, come on, get in the car." He stood up and the ice pack fell to the floor and the tea towel around it unfolded.

"What's going on, darling?"

"Inverloch. Evacuation."

"Are you sure?"

"Yes."

"I think it was a different town," I said. "I didn't hear Inverloch."

Just then the radio announcer repeated the names.

"Lynbrook, darling, near Pakenham."

"Oh, okay."

He sat back down again, listening intently to the broadcast. My grandmother picked up the ice pack, wrapped it again and put it back on his thigh.

It became a joke. Every time the radio said Lynbrook he would say "Inverloch?" and my grandmother would say "Lynbrook" and they would both smile.

"Inverloch?"

"Lynbrook, darling."

"Inverloch?"

"Lynbrook, darling."

But Strewth, what if they did call Inverloch? Neither of them were in any position to drive, but they wouldn't trust me to do it. Where would we go? What if we made a wrong turn into the fire?

. . .

They had grown up on the North Coast of Tasmania without electricity, met as children, and were married during the War. My grandfather had a service exemption due to being in medical school in Melbourne. They lived from dray carts to space travel, married for nearly seven decades. They were proud people. Had inherited frugal Welsh ways even though she had been one of the first women to graduate in science at the University and her father had been a Tasmanian MLC. I learned this not from her, but from my aunt. At age twelve my grandfather too went on scholarship to boarding school where his mother sent him sardines and cigarettes every week.

He hit me once when I must have been about eight or nine. We were in the front garden waving goodbye to some visitors departing in a car when a jump-jack stung my foot. I guess he didn't like how long or how loud I was carrying on for. He probably did it to save me from self-pity more than anything. My parents never hit me and I suppose I should see this as some sort of traumatic episode, but it wasn't. It was something of a window to a different world.

There was a knock on the door.

It was Gabe, the next-door neighbour, and he was offering us the use of his air-conditioned sitting room. By now, you may guess what my grandmother said to him.

"No thanks, we're right."

"Are you sure?"

"Oh yes."

"Well, let me know if you change your mind."

"Thanks Gabe."

And she shut the door on our salvation.

I tried to read a book but couldn't focus. Grandma tried to play the piano, but her hands grew too heavy. I went through the tables of contents of the stack of *Overland* magazines they had in the closet, glancing at the first paragraph of anything that looked interesting. But I couldn't finish a single piece. I had to focus on deep breathing and the sweat began trickling into my eyes. It was heat like the inside of the sun-dried tomato maker we'd given them that Christmas, like the tip of an electric drill after you've unscrewed twenty bolts from a couch, like the fore berth of a yacht on a sunny day, ligament-melting, eye-searing heat. I was twenty and I couldn't imagine how a ninety-year-old would manage.

"Oh, let's have something else," my grandmother said. "Let's put on some music."

"You do it," my grandfather said.

"I don't know what you want."

"I don't care. It's too hot."

"Alright."

It was hard to believe all the CDs hadn't melted, but she put on a collection of Uillean pipes; *O'Sullivan's March* was the first track. I knew the story of how O'Sullivan's party had walked the length of Ireland, fighting in their rear the whole way, keeping the women and children inside a circle of men, fording rivers and never ceasing through the night to walk, until a bedraggled few survivors fetched up in Donegal. Survival. In the high martial spirit of the song, you would never guess what it commemorated.

It occurred to me that what I felt then was similar to how I had felt just a few days previously, at a party with some friends from uni, sitting on a couch suddenly in a state of drunkenness where I had to focus my entire being on breathing, sitting upright, and holding the contents of my stomach. This was the first time I had experienced this, something my grandmother, who retained her Puritan habits without the Puritan God of her ancestors, would have disdained.

That was how I felt in the stifling back room. The fans were doing nothing more than blowing hot air around and my ice pack had warmed to the room's temperature. Where should we go? The library? The little supermarket? I didn't trust that they could make it to the car, let alone drive in this heat. I trusted myself to drive, but they would never allow it and an argument could kill. Maybe we could just sit in the car with its air-conditioning going. But surely that would be a terribubble waste.

· · ·

"Grandma, I'd like to go over to Gabe's for a bit. I think you should come. Sit in the air-conditioning. It's too hot."

"Oh, no, we're alright here."

I went out into the oven. I don't believe I would have had the energy to walk all the way down this driveway and then back up Gabe's driveway to the front door. I held the wires of the fence apart and stooped bow-legged through. Inside Gabe's sitting room it was cool, and he gave me mineral water with ice. I felt my mind revive.

"Gabe," I said. "I think if you go over and invite them for a cup of tea, they will come. Don't say anything about the air-conditioning or the heat."

It worked. A few minutes later I held the wire in the fence down for them, like inviting them into a forbidden paddock, and we sat in the cool drinking iced sparkling water. Gabe asked my grandfather to tell him about his time as a flying doctor in the Simpson Desert, refilling his glass with every question. When the cool change hit at about six o'clock we thanked Gabe and went home, again stooping through the wires of the fence. My grandmother and I opened all the blinds and all the doors and windows of the house. We sat in the gusts and the light eating cold chicken and beetroot. When we finished eating, we walked down to the beach and watched the golden sun filigree the hot grey clouds as it went down, bathing the trees and scrub Grandma had planted along the foreshore decades ago in warm light. I felt that satisfying all-body weariness that comes after a whole day of hiking.

. . .

It was only later we heard the stories of people boiled alive in their dams, noses burnt off, or trapped in cars on roads blocked by flaming trees. Kangaroos on fire bounding through towns. One man saw out the fire in a creek next to a lyrebird that had jumped in beside him. All the boundaries of life dissolved.

My grandfather stayed in bed most of the next day. His decline into death had begun, although it was a long month of suffering and lingering before we lost him, in the same back room, while my grandmother tried to put pillows under his back while he hacked and wheezed and convulsed into death. It had begun, I thought, with the moment the radio announcer said "Lynbrook" and he started from his chair.

# MR. HUMBERSTONE'S TRIAL

## I.

It was an eerily percussive aubade for Mr. Humberstone as he lay under his duck-down doona and flannel sheets this frosty July morning. He had woken at eight to the alarm he had forgotten to turn off, and without thinking of the reason why he was in his childhood bed—feet pressed uncomfortably against the headboard—he had fallen back into dreams as the gutter runoff slapped against the top of the tarps covering the bikes outside his window. In his dream he was in St. Peter's Basilica in Rome, arguing with Oliver Cromwell, who was up a ladder knocking a plaster Saint Sebastian off a cornice with a hammer. The ladder was shiny and modern, collapsible. Cromwell had the portly stature, ragged beard, and red face of Mr. Burnham, who had been Mr. Humberstone's year-twelve maths teacher. In the middle of the argument it all spun out again.

Lately Mr. Humberstone had imagined himself existing at key points in the past. For the last two of his twenty-seven years he had dwelt and devoted most of his autodidactic hours to the study of the emergence of the modern age, or, as Mr. Humberstone now preferred, the destruction—wanton, blind, idiotic—of Medieval grandeur and Christian civilisation. The Roman Empire was prologue, as he saw it, modernity epilogue. The meat was in the middle. The humanities had mainly inflicted suffering, the sciences had ameliorated the physical side of things but could still not answer the big questions of the mind and, dare it be said, the soul. Things were getting worse, there was no doubt about it.

Of course, he hadn't always known that that was what he was studying. He had passed what he thought of as his excusable Marxist phase and his liberal humanist phase and now had spent the last year crawling, a few knees and elbows at a time, drawn by an irresistible force, to Augustine, Aquinas, democracy of the dead, and eternal Christendom. The process had been slow, with many false starts, recidivism into favoured sins (Rawls, Foucault), desperate prayers, books by Kierkegaard, Feuerbach, Chesterton, John Milbank. No, it was clearly impossible, this Bible stuff. Things like that couldn't happen, the multiplying of the loaves and fishes, returning Lazarus to life. He would sigh with relief. But then what was left? Suddenly Mr. Humberstone found that there was nothing beneath his feet but God and the third person of the Trinity breathing life into his lungs and the second person closing and opening the ventricles of his heart between what he envisioned as the divine thumb and forefinger.

"Oh shit," he thought. "I'm a Christian. Oh shit, oh shit, shit, shit, shit."

"I cooked these at nine. They're cold." His mother proffered a plate of bacon and eggs through the door, balanced on her outstretched hand. It was now eleven-thirty, and Mr. Humberstone's grace period was over as far as she was concerned. The present, the spavined present, thudded down. It was going to be a hard day.

"I'm going to lunch," his mother said. "I'll be back around three."

"Mum, do you still have the shotgun?"

"Why do you ask?"

"Just wondering."

"It's in my closet."

As the events of the previous day stirred in his head—the blur of the train to Central, then buses—Wollongong—Cootamundra—Young. Then the walk in the rain to Ullathornes Road—the swinging gate, the calls that went straight to voicemail, those black letters on his front door, still dripping—he had a strange thought about the power of thoughts. The power of the thought of a single genius to inflict suffering or comfort on future generations. Like Newton and gravity or Descartes and "cogito, ergo sum." No wonder the Lord cared about your thoughts. Under any test of natural justice, it had been utterly correct to burn Jan Hus at the stake. His thoughts were dangerous. A single thought can lead to immeasurable suffering: no wonder the Lord cares about them. Five centuries later the results of Hus's crime were plain to see: a society of denatured self-facilitating individuals quivering back and forth between desire and shame, cowardly little apes demanding rights, ignorant of their Creator.

Mr. Humberstone began to look underneath the words. Lenin was uppermost in his mind. *Freedom of expression.* Who, Whom, remained unbeaten as a means to clarify thought. Power is. Not only power is, but God also is. Therefore, every society is a theocracy. Figure out what people have made into God, and their society snaps into focus. Fit people into clergy and laity. Sort events into liturgy and festival and communion and you had a pretty decent idea of what that society was. "Covers social inequality for *Sunday Life*" is the same as saying "Investigates miracles for the Vatican." Mr. Humberstone wanted to found a publishing house. The most anti-modern name possible. Ten Commandments Press, Genesis Publishing, Inquisition Press, Eight Hundred Degrees Books: *The temperature at which heretics burn.*

No, I am not an enlightened person, thought Mr. Humberstone. The reverie pulled him through a wormhole back to the present and the crime of which he had been accused, the reason he was listening to his mother fussing in the kitchen and not in his share-house scrolling through the overnight internet activity from America, theory and practice not yet being united in him, the enormity of it all, the danger he was in.

Mr. Humberstone removed his bedding and sprang up into the cold. He left the plate of bacon and eggs on the bedside table. In the kitchen he ground coffee and prepared the French press. To achieve optimum water temperature, he cut the boiling water with a splash from the tap and poured the contents of the kettle against the side of the cylinder.

While he drank the coffee, he checked his phone. The president of the United States was in Cuba; Mr. Humberstone was back home. He still had not answered Father Morphy's text from the night before, asking if he was okay as he had missed catechism class again.

"Sorry Father, had to rush back out to Young. Family dramas. See you next week."

The reply was instant: "Fine."

Still ravenous, Mr. Humberstone opened his mother's fridge to look for lunch. There was leftover tuna salad in a white bowl covered hastily with plastic wrap, which prompted him to think of John Donne: If a fish eats a loose bit of flesh from your finger, how will the atoms that were digested in the fish's stomach return to you at the final resurrection?

He went to the firebox, placed two skinny logs on either side and filled the space between them with crumpled newspaper from the opinion section of *The Australian*. Who is stacking her wood for her these days, he wondered. He gathered some twigs from outside that he placed on top of the newspaper and capped the structure with a flat log. The twigs were damp, but he knew from experience they would catch and he enjoyed the hiss of their steam. He struck a match and set it to the bottom of the newspaper. Closing the door, he opened the flue all the way. After five minutes he put in another log and watched the flames rise at the back of the box. Inside, a movement caught his eye. On the near, unburnt side of the wood, was a small huntsman, the same colour as the wood, moving one of its front legs up and down slowly as if testing the heat of the flames rising on the opposite side of its log. He opened the firebox door for the huntsman, which had clung to the doorframe.

"Mum is just going to kill you later," he said.

"Thanks all the same," replied the spider, scuttling away under the kindling box.

Mr. Humberstone opened his notebook and began to write to Marley.

Dear Marley,

Can I explain my conversion? Ask a man why he loves the music he loves. In a way, I can, in a way, I can't. You will decide, of course, as you must. You will never see inside of my brain, or see the things, however trivial, just the way I saw them. More importantly, you will never know, unless a great miracle occurs, the people I knew and what they showed me. They are impressive people, these Christians, us Christians, some of them anyway, and only at certain times, like all of us.

I can assure you that I saw no miracles. Nothing from the heavens shouted down with wisdom and proved its presence afterward with a searing token. Though I suspect he has, to this day I cannot be certain that God has ever spoken to me. How would I know? Yes, I had the example, as you mentioned, of poetry and architecture. Hopkins, Arnold, our own Les Murray: sure they are impressive, and I am now convinced that no poets are atheists, but poetry is surely not enough. And cathedrals: who can understand how they are made? To me they are permanent as the valleys and the mountains are permanent. It is important to understand that what we mean by supernatural phenomena are merely natural phenomena which we have yet to understand. Of course, to say this is to say in another way that natural phenomena that we do understand such as rain, wind, growth of crops, are also supernatural. In other words, everything we see is supernatural, God's hand is in everything.

No, this isn't making sense, thought Mr. Humberstone. Lots of people like poetry, even Christian poetry, without converting. He remembered how strange it was to find that the proceedings of Wycliffe's trial, for example, suddenly concerned him. All the proclamations, coronations, and wars of Europe took on immediacy. Do I agree with Calvin here? Did William of Ockham pave the way—however naively—for positivism, empiricism, and modernity? Did Saint Thomas Aquinas likewise lay the foundations for the eradication of the simple faith of love with his precise inductions?

His phone lit up with a call from his editor. He let it ring out and then checked the message.

"Callum," said the editor's voice, attempting to sound normal. "We're just wondering what you're up to. Be good to touch base. I'm sure you know what I mean. Ring me back, please."

He called his housemate Aaron.

"Aw g'day mate, has any mail arrived for me?"

"Nah, don't think so mate, but I'll keep a look out."

"Okay, cheers mate."

II.

RAPIST. The word was painted at eye level in six-inch black letters on the bright red door of Mr. Humberstone's Newtown share-house. Painted with a brush, rather neatly, not sprayed; thin drips of black ran down the door. To think that it had stared at his back as he went down the front walk out to catch the train in to work that morning. Although there were three other young men who lived in the house, Mr. Humberstone knew that the authoritative word was meant for him, knew by intuition how it had come about, if not exactly who had painted those neat yet overflowing letters.

His editor had sent him home. "You can't be here at the moment, I'm sorry," he said, then seeing Mr. Humberstone's face, he added, "Oh, you poor thing, have you not seen?"

Marley had made a tweet thread detailing an unwanted encounter. His name was not mentioned, but there was more than enough detail, including about his workplace, to identify him. The original tweet had over one thousand likes and several hundred retweets as well as replies and quote tweets detailing suspicions, dark hints, and rumours about him. It was Aaron who suggested he should probably leave the city. He said it with an edge that suggested Aaron wanted him gone, for the sake of peace in the house, but Mr. Humberstone was not in a state to register such subtleties.

Marley had been a source of comfort to him, primarily, a friendly face he could go to at the cold end of the night. She worked in the university library putting books back on the shelves, cataloguing new acquisitions, and waking up sleeping students at the communal tables. She had sought him out originally after he had made a number of unusual requests for books from off-site storage—books that hadn't been checked out for thirty years, or in a few cases, never—and she recognised his name from the newspaper. Naturally he had returned again and again without ever making it clear what was happening. She, as well, liked to keep things vague. Something about him advised against getting too close. But he was tall. So tall, and up in his own world up there, wrapped in his cloudy thoughts, or hunched over a book, head working like an oil pump.

And then all of a sudden, after one of their regular evenings—it had been perhaps three months since their first—just as the spring was breaking in Sydney—she fell hard. It was seeing him at a party actually, nothing he said to her. Seeing him at a party giving out book recommendations to two girls she didn't know, who were gazing up at his clouds, open-mouthed in amazement like groupers.

One weekend they flew to Melbourne together for her friend's exhibition opening at a gallery in Collingwood. There was free wine and beer at the gallery. He was talking to one of her friends about the differences between panhandlers in Melbourne and Sydney (in Sydney they are utterly abject, slumped on the sidewalk; in Melbourne they're polite and usually offer their gifts, say, playing the harmonica, or rapping), when an argument struck up between Mr. Humberstone and three women friends of Marley's artist friend.

Even the most level-headed arguments are hard to repeat. Tone of voice and volume account for too much; opposing points are ignored. They aren't like conversations in books. The artist might have said something like, "That's the problem with euthanasia:

it's fine as a principle, but the safeguards are impossible." Mr. Humberstone would have agreed. The lack of music may have been responsible for what was said subsequently.

"So why are you against euthanasia?" This came from a girl who was standing over her seated friend with her arms around her friend's neck.

"Are you serious?"

"They're the same thing, just at different times of life."

"I can create life and take it away. I would kill myself to abort a baby."

"What a tawdry idea of what a human being is."

"I believe everyone has a right to decide when to end their own life."

"Why? You didn't decide when to start your life."

"The world is overpopulated already," said another girl.

"Whoa, careful there, you're heading into Mengele territory. You don't want to go there," Mr. Humberstone said.

"Excuse me, have you ever watched your grandmother die of Alzheimer's? Have you? Have you? I did. She should have died two years earlier." She was crying now and had moved over to lean into Mr Humberstone's face.

"Uh, are you going to listen to my argument?"

"I want to know if you've ever watched your grandmother die in front of you."

With a combination of desperate curiosity and immediate horror, Marley listened to what Mr. Humberstone then said.

"I watched my Dad die of cancer in front of me when I was nine years old, thank you very much, but I'm not trying to put that on you." He had raised his voice considerably to speak over the crying girl and the commotion of the street, and he had put Mengele on her.

"Don't raise your voice to me," she said. She screamed something else about the male will to dominate, and, as her friends began to take her away, what sounded like *sexist bigot* or *sexist begone.*

"Oh, let it out. Let it out," he said.

They got another drink. "Pathetic," he said, "imagine if her grandmother could see her using her to win an argument."

But later, after a few more drinks, it was his turn to cry, prompted by that memory he had spoken into being. He cried as he walked the rainy streets of Fitzroy with Marley back home. "Fuck her sob story," he said. "You should never trade off it."

· · ·

Back in Sydney, the first bad signs came when she had just gotten out of hospital. The removal of a cyst had gone poorly. He sent her a stuffed bear with BRAVE emblazoned across its chest and wrote her a card. She went straight to his house.

"Hey, sorry," he said. "I have a last-minute meeting with a source. Been trying to arrange this for ages. You'll have to go."

And she cried and cried and thought back over those nights and how she had done so much for him—made him poached eggs in the morning, stolen that Berdyaev book that was going for two hundred and eighty dollars on Amazon from the library, which he still hadn't read, listened to him complain about his mother. How she felt as though the more she wanted him the more he slipped away, and that she could no more leave him alone and hope he would come to her than annoy him with her feelings. She knew acting would be futile and yet she could not do nothing.

So, she found herself outside his window that same night and then in his bed.

"Are you resisting me for religious reasons?" she asked.

"You could say that. It's just—while I'm in catechesis I don't want to disappoint Father Morphy."

He didn't tell her about his vision from the last time they were together. After she left on that happier morning, he re-read *The Man Who Was Thursday* and began to feel strange when he came to the line near the end, "No agonies can be too great to buy the right to say to this accuser, 'we also have suffered.'" He finished the book and began reading the Bible. The uneasy feeling continued, and he prayed the rosary and went to bed at 10 p.m. He awoke exactly at midnight, having experienced the most terrifying dream of his life. Usually his nightmares took the form of physical destruction—watching his skin melt off his hand was the most common recurring event—but in this dream he was not destroyed. He walked through rooms in an infinite house with creatures varying from normal human to demon to animal and all possible amalgamations of the three. The scariest was a kind of insect-human that reminded him of Dante's *Inferno* when the man and the lizard fuse in the eighth circle.

Marley deleted the tweets two days later, but there remained the screenshots, which circulated among the supportive tweets from their common friends and digital acquaintances, as well as archly phrased questions about his whereabouts directed at his employer. The ball was rolling.

III.

Mr. Humberstone dreamed he was giving his maiden speech to Parliament. He spoke with that orchestral fluency that comes just before and after deep sleep, in that twilight of trance that writers mourn when they awake, staring at their mundane page with its paltry scratches, splutterings, crossings out.

"Mr. Speaker, Honourable Members, Ladies and Gentlemen, I stand before you today in total opposition to the processes and principles that brought me to this place. Yes, Australian democracy has failed. Democracy has failed wherever it has been tried. Without the veneer of technological advance, obtained by the undemocratic efforts of a few thousand talented men, the period from the French Revolution until now would look like a moonscape of emotional misery, economic poverty, and spiritual corruption. Mr. Speaker, democracy stands condemned on the altar of history. I advocate the immediate restoration of full sovereignty to Her Majesty Elizabeth the Second. Mr. Speaker, in condemning mob rule I stand with the best minds of history, Plato, Marcus Aurelius, Thomas Jefferson, and Metternich, among countless others. I make this pledge to the people who placed their trust in me to represent the cause of just and intelligent and true order in Australia. The first act of the Inquisition Party when we win government will be to withdraw from all international human rights treaties, repeal the Crimes Act, and replace it with sections 46-74 of canon law of the Roman Catholic Church and put witches and warlocks to the torch. I will not vote on any motion put before this dangerous and illegitimate house. I swear fealty to her Majesty Queen Elizabeth the Second and await her instruction and guidance in all matters put forward for my attention . . . When the vile Regicide occurred . . ."

Mr. Humberstone woke up with a dead left leg. His left foot was pressed against the footboard. He rolled over gingerly and dropped the leg out of the doona and over the side.

A feeling of psychic weight that he could only describe as oppression by God came upon him, yet he knew that even the thought was blasphemous. God was a gentleman who did not force himself on you. Let no man say that God is tempting him into sin. Sometimes he avoided God for a few hours of relaxation, and he thought that all that was over, that he could go back to pleasant life. But of course, there was nothing else except atoms and he rushed back to God in fear. There was no middle path. Mr. Humberstone felt like a man diving into a snowdrift for relief from the sauna and back again.

He went into his mother's room and opened the closet. It was there, barrel down, leaning against a low set of white drawers, the shotgun. He checked the chamber: unloaded, of course. What was he expecting?

Mr. Humberstone knew what the problem was. He was pursuing a subjective state of well-being through the feeling of faith. The important thing was to know that God was real no matter what he thought. Knowing this did not make him feel better.

He remembered something Marley had said in one of their arguments: "Jesus was a phony. The Golden Rule is bullshit. What about BDSM? Treat others how you want to be treated, sure. But others aren't you and they don't want to be treated like you. And what if you hate yourself? Are you meant to hate others then?"

For all the vividness of his imagination, he could not imagine other people going to Hell. God would understand them, did already understand them (of course), and would forgive them. They were in a form of invincible ignorance. But for himself he made no such excuse. No, he couldn't imagine anyone he knew going to Hell, except his mother. He feared for her and prayed for the scales to fall and for God to take her with Him.

How could you hold on to the medieval view in this day and age? How could you go back to it, once you started down Descartes's street? But here he was. Pobedonostsev was right. Every single sentence was true, everything bad he predicted came to pass, yet life rolled on. Cataclysm. All the great lollipop ladies standing in the middle of the road screaming stop were all correct, every single catastrophe the traditionalists of the past had warned against had occurred, but the buildings still stood and somehow the light next to Mr. Humberstone's bed switched on when he wanted to read.

He prayed. "Lord, please help me to love others. Please help resolve this situation in the best possible way. I pray for Marley, for her welfare . . . for my mother."

IV.

He sat outside in the backyard drinking coffee. The sun shone down, but the wind blew hard, and away down the road the clouds were bubbling. The sinfonia of Bach's Partita No. 2 for Harpsichord was on replay in his head. He began writing again, this time to Aaron, who had watched from start to finish.

Mate,

Becoming a Catholic means learning to see the world as the huge miracle. You had to train yourself to be a medieval person who could see everything in the world as a sentient being or constituent of a larger sentient being. Order, hierarchy, and unity. Essence and substance. Sure, Catholics don't face persecution in Australia but we face social ridicule. Why do you think I don't tell people at parties? Marley doesn't get it. My mother doesn't get it.

Everyone's like, 'as long as it works for you.' What does that even mean? I work for it. It's not piecemeal: I'll have a little resurrection, hold the demons and exorcisms, oh and yeah—the gays are all right now. It's not like a buffet. Imagine a psychologist saying: well, you know, Freud just really works for me. Or a philosopher saying, Nietzsche just fits with my worldview. No, it's the opposite. I was always a Catholic.

If I may plunge so deep so quickly, I think you should know about something I feel we've lost in the modern world, a true sense of the ineffable, the absolute, without which—though money and political stability can float us for a while, perhaps a long while, perhaps through many, many generations—we are lost. Lost in the deepest sense, without knowing why. It's a sense I think, if you are honest with yourself, you will feel as you grow up. It will fill you if you don't fill it. The trouble is that just about anything can fill it. A person, a woman can fill it, you may fill it in her. It's hardest to learn the damage of that, that damaging the others you care most for is inevitable. So, I guess that's what this is about, to try to get you to fill it with something permanent and good. It is the most paradoxical because it must come from within you, yet it exists whether you believe it or not. My father always told me I had to be grateful, which was a good enough idea. He didn't tell me who to or what for.

The wind picked up and drove him inside, where he continued writing on the couch:

She's like, this is going to require compromise and I'm like yes it will but all the compromise is going to be on my end. I still haven't told Morphy about her. That's another thing: she's like why do you have to talk to a priest about it?

The harpsichord stopped and Aaron's voice broke in:

"It's a bit of a headfuck when your boyfriend decides that the most intimate thing you do together is a mortal sin, I mean . . . "

"Okay. Possibly."

"Did you try to get her involved with your beliefs?"

"I asked her to pray the rosary with me. Showed her how to do it, explained what everything was. We did it together and at the end she's still like, this is bullshit, why do you have to do it ten times, why can't you only do it once? She tried to sneak in the Proddy bit on the end of the Our Father, nah you don't do that. I can explain that there are different things you're meant to think about as you go through it but she's still going to say this is bullshit. We had a big fight about it and the only way I could get her to shut up about it was to, you know, give her what she wanted. And I thought this is just one more sin I'll have to confess before Easter."

Aaron did not reply to this.

He started another essay:

I know someone in real life who is a technological Calvinist. He believes that when you die people from the future instantly whisk you there, where the cure for your disease or the device for your bodily failure is readily available. All worldly problems have been sorted. Nanotechnology has cured cancer, AIDS, and the need to work. The fusion of human brain with mechanical body has been perfected. Any desire can be fulfilled at the press of a button on a three-dimensional printer. They invented time travel, for God's sake. 'Everyone goes on holidays all the time; basically, you just live and . . . basically, explore,' this friend of mine said. Not everyone, mind. The people from the future scout around for the good eggs. Someone's probably judging you right now. You never know who might be from the future, so you have to watch what you say and be nice to everyone.

What, I ask, is the point of that? I agree with Borges's vision of immortality: a great deal of boredom followed by a great deal of nothing followed by squalor. That drop of mercury irreducible in the human brain. This is the problem with religions that preach an afterlife. Heaven and Hell will eventually become indistinguishable. Unless they exist in such a way as to be completely beyond human comprehension, which I concede is possible, perhaps even likely.

VI.

It happened on his second night in Young. His mother was preparing dinner while watching the news. "An editor from a Sydney-based newspaper is accused of improper conduct towards a cadet journalist. It is alleged that the accused, who can't be named for legal reasons, repeatedly assaulted the alleged victim in a Newtown home over the course of several weeks . . . "

Mr. Humberstone's mother raised her eyebrows and turned to face her son. "How about that?" she said.

"Mmhm."

"It's everywhere."

"Yes Mum," Mr. Humberstone sighed.

"How's that?"

"It's fine, Mum."

"It's all right. I believe you."

"What?"

"Janet at the refugee centre told me. Her son is the photographer for the *Herald*, remember?"

"I didn't do it, obviously."

"Yes Call-o. Jesus. Oh, sorry baby."

"It's okay, Mum."

"You stay as long as you need."

He was put on half-pay. He did a bit of editing and commissioning of writers he already knew. His editor thought it best to keep his byline out. His ideas piled up. He found that the web recommended articles like "Five Stocks Perfect for Your 70s" and "Why Gold Is Set to Soar." The world knew he needed security, or the world knew he was afraid. And why shouldn't you be afraid, thought Mr. Humberstone. Afraid for your soul above all. It was assailed from all sides. He called Aaron every day to see if the charges had arrived. And each day of that winter Mr. Humberstone spent in like manner.

VII.

One morning in early spring as the rain spattered the same tarp outside Mr. Humberstone's window, his dreams were cut short by his mother, who stood over him.

"Come help me bring these boxes for the refugees in from the car."

"Yeah, okay."

She had filled the car up with bulk supplies from the warehouse store in Cowra. She and Mr. Humberstone made up food and toiletries packages in bags that the community group had sewn out of old curtain fabric, towels, and unworn clothes. In went the tinned sardines, salmon, soap, and toilet paper.

"Their stories are so sad. It makes me grateful to be here and have what we have."

"Okay, Mum."

"Gautam, he's the one who's been cutting up my firewood, was kidnapped to be a soldier when he was eight in Sri Lanka, but he escaped and the family had to flee with nothing. They've been in camps for fifteen years."

"It's not that you'll never be able to appreciate their deprivations, it's that you'll never be able to appreciate their pleasures."

"What? Sweetie, I just want you to do something while you're here."

"I'm writing."

"I know, but something else. Why don't you talk to Mr. Harvey who owns the timber yard? He could get you working with Gautam. You still remember how to use the chainsaw?"

"Yes, of course I do."

"Do you want me to arrange it?"

"No. But if you do, fine."

And so she did. Was this not just another cliché? The cerebral man finding redemption in hard labour? But it worked: the fatigue in his hands, his lower back, and his right shoulder; the pleasures of food and drink and sinking into the sofa heightened by the soreness in his chest and legs.

IX.

One Sunday in the spring, he was received into the Church in Young by Father Seneviratne, with Gautam as his sponsor.

"I've explained your situation and the progress you made in Sydney. The bishop says it's fine, as long as you make confession of course."

"Father, I didn't do it."

"No of course, I mean general confession."

Before Mass that Sunday, Mr. Humberstone knelt and wept and the tears came down and the statue of the Virgin stared down, visibly unmoved. Framed under the nave, holding the candlesticks he had just polished, Father Seneviratne trembled and waited.

God, the source of all. The revelation of Christ, proof of God's love and fidelity. The forgiveness of sins. How ecstatic Mr. Humberstone felt, his glutes and thighs shivered and hardened to an uncontrollable tremble, as when he had first believed. The light wind that morning blew in the love of God. "I'm sorry, Lord. Thank you, Lord." It was all paid for, now and forever—his blasphemy, arrogance, and despair wiped away.

When the weather turned hot, he took the bus back to the city. He stayed in a backpacker's and worked the 5 a.m. shift at the Wynyard Station KFC. Walking by his old house, he saw not a trace of the word on the door. They had matched the paint exactly.

# COMPLINE

Week six of the fourth lockdown. The beginning of August, under steel clouds which selfishly withhold rain. You are sick of playing chess alone in your room in the rectory, listening to the clicking of the traffic crossings, clicking so the blind can find them. No one told them curfew is 8 p.m. Scrolling on your phone in your chair by the window, you see in the corner park on the other side of the street, the schizo from the free Wednesday lunch zipping and unzipping his tent flap like a child who just discovered how it works. The playground equipment is adorned with red and white police tape and a big corflute declaring the park closed. Standing at the radiator, lifting a dumbbell. Window, radiator, dumbbell, and back again. The same night after night. Father O'Riordan on the couch with a glass of wine, Alfred in the next room posting Lord-knows-what online in between endless sets of push-ups, and Francisco across the hall constantly on the phone with his family in Colombia. You once checked the time difference and found it was between three and four in the morning over there and Francisco was just happily chatting away with his mum and sister on speakerphone. Night after night. It's all you can do to focus on a page or two of the *Rule of Benedict* ("essential for curates") that Father O'Riordan gave you.

A story pops up on your phone about politicians caught at a party near the Parliament building, breaking their own rules. Dan in the chat group says, "Everyone else will be fine: diseases can't jump species like that." You had been wracking your brain trying to come up with a way to have a party. Plenty are willing to come but no one to host. Seeing the story, your background rage bubbles up, like a crude oil strike from an inexhaustible seam, spouting high into the air. Action must be taken. Fear is a sin. And then it hits you like an idea for a story cascading out all at once from somewhere above you: the choir vestry. The perfect place. It is tucked away on the opposite side of the church. All you would have to do is go out the side door of the rectory, walk behind the church, and then discreetly open the gate to allow guests in off the street. Once you're in there, the space is generous, high-ceilinged, wood-floored; it will hold you all. You won't even be technically going out of your living space. If guests arrive one by one, no one will notice—not that there would be anyone out and about that time of night anyway. You could even have some music.

There were security cameras installed after the Christ statue in the memorial garden was toppled by a schizo—a different one from the one outside your window, one of many that patrol the neighbourhood—but there should be no reason for Father O'Riordan to check them. A nice, mature gathering. Father O'Riordan would never know. Did not Saint Benedict write that "God often reveals what is better to the younger"?

Jesse is the most keen. And if he shows up, the others will too. The messages go out to Carlo, Luke, James, and Dan, all of whom can hold their liquor. Alfred and Francisco? No, too much of a liability. Best to keep secrets outside the household. Saturday at about 10 o'clock, subject to Father O'Riordan's bedtime, is the appointed time. The days fly by. After dinner on the designated night, you sweep and mop the stairs as part of your weekly chores assigned by Father O'Riordan. Normally you hate the drudgery. Doing this manual work, contrary to what all the monastics say, brings out the free range of your emotions—self-pity to rage and back again, although really what's the difference? It's always seemed pointless to clean things like stairs and floors. Windows and mirrors, yes, but things that we tread upon? They will just get dirty again, often straight away from the footprints the cleaner leaves behind. But tonight the anticipation carries you through.

To get out the back door you have to pass Father O'Riordan on the couch, slumped and twisted like a cooked lobster watching TV with his glass of wine: this priest with boundless energy, who brought you into the church, who is so suited to his inner urban parish, able to converse with publicans and blue-haired, nose-pierced university students who come into the church's op shop. You remember how in between lockdowns one of the local publicans—an atheist from where, oh right, from Sweden, no less—allowed a Sunday Mass in his beer garden because the rules stipulated that only twenty-five were allowed in "places of worship" but one hundred could gather in a pub, all on the back of the charisma of this set-apart man. How he is inviting and welcoming without compromising on the essentials of belief; how he took the parish from dying to full in a few short years, how he did it without guitar masses for the old folks or coddling the young, how he always wears full clerical dress in a neighbourhood where half the people would assume he is on his way to a costume party and the other half would wear a look saying "pedophile" louder than any accusatory shout; how lightly he has carried it all, the dinners with Alfred and Francisco, the gin and tonics, the belonging, the going across to the church together for compline; how you had heard the snide remarks—"Father O'Riordan is trying to build a monastery in his house"; how you wanted to follow in his footsteps as a soldier for Christ, illuminating the dead hordes of your city and country; how no better adventure could be imagined. What a waste of his gifts it seems now, to see him lying there reclining on the couch like a leftover chicken breast, churning through some corny detective comedy program. It is this waste of life, you tell yourself, that justifies your rage.

"Just going across to pray," you say. "It's my mother's year's mind tomorrow."

He turns back to the analgesic screen.

You wave at the hematite eye of the camera mounted on the side of the church before unlocking the gate and propping it open with a bluestone brick. You prop open the door of the choir vestry with a stool. You find a box of votive candles in the cabinet next to the sink, light one, and place it on the stool. The new red-light district, you think. You put on Carols from Kings on your bluetooth speaker. Photos of the church ladies' cricket team from the 1920s stare down from the walls. What is this slinking about in the dark when you should be shouting the truth from the rooftops?

As you wait you check the news of the lockdown protest in the city. Dan had invited you along, and you told him you would go, but then there was an email from the Archbishop's office. "Archdiocese clergy and staff are reminded to avoid any gatherings which may undermine public health measures currently in place . . ." The rage kicks in, but no: it would not be worth jeopardising your selection conference for ordination in a few months' time. Pepper spray, rubber bullets, a few thousand troublemakers—the headlines say.

Jesse arrives on his bicycle with his food delivery hot bag on his back. It's how he's been getting around curfew. Cops won't stop delivery riders. He's brought a six pack of Cooper's stout.

"Padre's still awake, so I couldn't bring any drinks."

"No wuckers."

"Where's James? I thought he was coming with you."

"He bitched out."

"Gay."

"Yeah."

Jesse twists the cap off a stout and passes it to you.

"Cheers. To freedom."

"To freedom."

Carlo arrives with a sign.

"I brought you a present."

It's the corflute from the playground. There are holes in the corners where Carlo had ripped it from its zip-tied fastness.

"Fantastic. Unbelievable stuff."

"Bro, what's up with your hair?" Jesse asks.

"I haven't had a haircut because I'm an enemy of the state."

"Nice."

"Can I change the music?" Carlo asks.

"No, only hymns tonight."

Luke arrives with a bottle of red. His father is dying in Brisbane and he can't visit. A solemnity, which you can't help but savour, combined with a pride that you are able to give him at least this, give him something, comes over you. This is life, this is death. The rising voices of the boys singing "I saw three ships come sailing in . . ." mingle with the novelty of company. The mingling makes you elated, energised with beer and banter. The thrill of mutual incrimination. You have a second stout, then a third, then some long pulls from Luke's wine. Jesse lights some coals in the thurible. Incense suffuses the room.

Dan arrives, limping. He totters in the doorway, leans against the doorframe, swings his left leg over the threshold. He needs a beer. He looks exhausted.

"Fucking rubber bullets," he says.

He pulls up his left pant leg to reveal an enormous bruise on his calf—looks like a blue and purple fried egg in a pan, almost like the eye of a peacock feather.

"Got me here too." He opens his overcoat and lifts up his shirt. A smaller bruise spreads across his ribs.

"Fuck, how was it?"

"Incredible. Must have been a hundred thousand or more. The whole city was blocked off."

"Channel seven says a few thousand."

"Fuck them."

"Yeah, fuck them."

"Anyway, how's Father?"

"Yeah, good, he's alright."

"I wanted to come, mate, but I just couldn't," you say.

"No worries, mate."

Jesse starts opening all the cupboards. He takes out and lights up an entire carton of tea candles. You are too tired to stop him. He puts on a cassock and hands them out to the others.

"No, put them back," you say.

But they don't.

"Okay, just as long as you put them back."

Another swig of Luke's bottle. You put on a cassock two sizes too big.

"Where are the chicks?" Jesse says.

"Lol."

"Someone should tell a story," you say.

"You."

"No."

"It has to be you, bro."

"No."

"Mate, it's your party."

"If you don't tell one, I'll tell one about you," says Jesse.

"All right, fine. Ready?"

Luke switches the Bluetooth speaker off. The candles and the clicking of the crosswalk buttons fills the silence.

"All right, fine. There once was a deacon named Nathan."

Jesse initiates a brief round of applause.

"He went on a trip to Barcelona. To visit his friend Cameron. Luke, you met my friend Cam, didn't you?"

"Don't think so."

"Get to the story."

"Anyway, Cam was on exchange at one of the unis there. This was many years ago. We went out on a Saturday night, or maybe it was just a weekday; I can't remember. We were with some of his friends from the uni, all exchange students, like him. It's funny, the cheap beer in Spain is called Estrella. Straya. There was this girl from Germany."

Jesse lets out a whoop.

"This girl from Germany. She kept insulting me. I would tell her about my history research that I was doing at that time, and she would say 'you are writing about dead people, it has no meaning.' Not that you choir boys would know this, but when a woman insults you it's a good sign. Anyway we went to a few different bars—remember bars?—and she said she hated me. Another good sign. I hope for the sake of the future of the Church you are all taking notes on this. I just laughed in her face and raised my drink. I don't know what time it was, but we ended up alone on the beach. We dipped our toes in the water, sat down on the sand. I asked her about Germany. We were just about to kiss, and I mean just about, right? Face to face, a millimetre apart, eyes closed, and then she jumps up and sprints back up the beach screaming."

You pause to take a sip of wine.

"This gypsy had been watching us and chose that moment to make off with her handbag. She had caught up to him and was yelling at him in German. He was just standing there about four feet tall. 'Kill him' she screamed at me. 'Kill him!' I took the bag off him and told her to check if everything was there. It was. 'Kill him!' she said. I said no. He didn't take anything. Who knows if he has friends around the corner. Neither of us speak Spanish. 'Okay, punch him.' Anyway, of course I didn't, and he wandered away and does this explain why I'm becoming a priest?"

Another quiet round of applause and a whistle from Jesse.

"All right, your turn. You've gotten your jollies."

You suddenly feel completely exhausted, with an ache growing at your temples.

Luke's phone had lit up in the middle of your story, and he had stepped out to take the call. He returns with the news that his father has died in Brisbane. He won't be able to go to the funeral or visit his family. The shock of the news, which—as you knew from your mother's death—never sinks in, flows through each of you. Something must be done. Somehow, supernaturally sobering up, you retrieve the compline booklets from the stalls in the sanctuary and lead the five in prayer. Dan follows along in the book but doesn't speak or sing.

*The Lord grant us a quiet night and a perfect end.*

It's a high-wire act getting through compline as your head is now throbbing, but you lean on the Lord.

"And we pray for the soul of Luke's father . . . "

"Matthew."

"Matthew."

*Grant eternal unto him, O Lord . . .*

From outside the door there comes a shout.

"What are you doing, you vegetable!"

And before you can get up from your seat there is the sound of ceramic fracturing. Dan, forgetting his limp, is out the door and by the time you get up to see what has happened he has the schizo on the ground with his arms behind his back. The schizo is screaming bloody murder, yelling "Vegetable! Vegetable! Vegetable!"

You and me both, brother. When the angel takes you by the scruff of the neck and points to your garbage heaps of sin, bellowing "explain!" you will say nothing and point to that man on the ground. The statue has fallen face down in the flower bed and broken in such a way as to appear elongated, like a wooden model laid out piece by piece before being assembled.

At the breakfast table after Mass (which, because of the restrictions, is offered at the same table only for the four residents of the rectory), Father O'Riordan says to you:

"Someone knocked over the statue of Our Lord in the memorial garden last night. I thought I remembered locking the gate, but I must have forgotten."

What will you say? That God reveals what is better to the younger? It could hardly be called a party, more of a gathering, a retreat, a refuge, an act of self-care. A response to circumstance, political conditions, social constructs. What about those politicians who did the same—how can men live like this? Hide me under the shadow of your wings.

"Again?" you say, stalling for time.

"Yes. Can you check the camera footage for me? Tell me what you see."

# McCAFFREY: BY AN OBITUARIST

Dear Editor,

Sure, I knew McCaffrey, at college, in first year, and once, once only, in the Biblical sense. That's why I can't write you an obituary of her, you understand. Or rather, this is my obituary, but you can't publish it like this—sorry about that. I'm sorrier still that she has died. The species is minus one great scientist and one great woman. There are no endings in a person's life except the last one, but the dead leave countless endings in their slipstreams. Chesterton remarked that a suicide doesn't only kill himself, he kills everyone. McCaffrey's death feels like that.

When I first saw Wendy McCaffrey out of my third-floor window, she was a mousey girl with clear green eyes and red bob who sat with her legs hunched up reading her textbooks by the light of the sun. Later, when McCaffrey became an eminent physicist and worked with the settlers at Asimov, I published her articles in *Scientific Australian*. They were published worldwide. She headed the team that developed the first viable method of growing crops on Mars and cracked the secret of forcing normal uptake of nutrients by roots in the weak Martian gravity.

Though there was plenty of Biblical knowledge around at college I was generally excluded, self-excluded, I should say. I never learned that the girls could be approached bluntly, a hangover from my Californian upbringing. I had somehow picked up the belief that unsuccessful approaches resulted in arrest warrants and therefore kept an agonizing distance between myself and women. Pretending not to care proved an unsuccessful strategy, until I met McCaffrey.

That wasn't the only way I was maladjusted. The college housed mostly students from the country (McCaffrey was from Horsham), and the subtleties of the male's speech—"Call cunts mate, call mates cunt," and all that—took me a while to pick up.

A month into first semester, I was invited around to the second-year block by a boy I'd become friendly with over the lunchtime table. The older students took a great effort to get to know everyone. It really was a friendly place. In the first weeks of term there was no such thing as being unwelcome at a dining table. This second-year boy, Dalt, short for Dalton, and his friends seemed to me more sophisticated than the drunk braggarts in my cohort. Those things were much more important to me then. I was reading Faulkner, Czesław Miłosz, and Philip Roth, and thought I had a unique angle of approach. When I arrived, McCaffrey was sitting at Dalton's desk wrapped in a sky-blue blanket. Dalt and his friends Horace and Dougie were sitting in their underwear on the single-sized bed under Dalt's doona. The three boys were all dark-haired but had sharply differing features. Dalt was large-nosed, thin-lipped; his face was triangle-shaped with the apex at his chin. Horace had compact features and facial hair like a wet towel around his chin. Dougie's head was shaped like a printed copy of *Anna Karenina*.

It wasn't a typical welcome.

"Hi Nathan, did you know that nothing three or more men do can be gay?" asked Dalt. He had these strange ideas which I was never quite sure if he believed or not.

"What if it's three gay guys?" I asked, ingratiating myself.

"No, not gay, it's just fooling around."

But it was an exciting welcome. At least they were discussing theories and ideas rather than drink or sport. I was handed a beer and sat down on the edge of the bed. McCaffrey and I were introduced. The five of us drank and smoked weed (Dalt took the batteries out of the smoke alarm, and we made a plan to burn frozen pies on his sandwich press if anyone got suspicious). I only had a few puffs, but I was gone. The three boys wrestled in bed while McCaffrey and I quietly made fun of them.

"Only a man can be a true feminist, because it entails sacrifice. Feminism for women is just self-interest." This was Dalt again. McCaffrey scoffed with such violence that the remnants of her mouthful of beer rained down on Dalt's desk.

Only a slave-owner can be an abolitionist, only a colonist can be a freedom fighter, only we can forgive ourselves. No, that's not quite right.

The boys passed out, and McCaffrey and I headed down the corridor to the stairwell. "Do you want to come check out my room?" I asked. She was suitably impressed by my growing library of novels, travelogues, and poetry. Her torso was straight-up and down, like an underarm crutch, and she had larger than average breasts with very pale pink nipples, and a small, white-girl's bum. When I leaned down to kiss her, her breath smelled like the bitter aftertaste of corn flakes and milk. I didn't know that Horace had ended a year-long relationship with McCaffrey just weeks before, nor that she still loved him. In due course I checked out her room. Horace and I talked about it only in junk time, at 2 or 3 a.m., when we were both paralytic. He would ask me how things were going with her and say "It's fine, man, I don't care. You're a good guy." I counted him a friend, as I did Dalt and Dougie. Dalt did philosophy and Dougie became a cop after finishing his neuroscience degree. Dark-haired

Horace studied music and was a gun guitar player in the college band. In fact, he could play just about any instrument passably.

McCaffrey and I went out on our own a few times (her heels wobbled in the blue-stone laneways), but usually I tagged along with her friends, or she came along with Dalt and the others, and of course there were the weekly college piss-ups. I let her invite me places and was woken by her messages at 3 a.m. asking to come to my room for a cuddle. I always seemed to keep more clothes on than her. She chided me about my lit essays, "Writing some satisfactory bullshit?" I hadn't the knowledge to chide her. I knew nothing about her schoolwork, the foundation that would later enable our (humanity's) first inter-planetary settlement.

Angles were important at college. Our brick buildings were from the sixties; old enough to feel settled, but next to the sandstone and bluestone colleges, hardly of account. There were six residential buildings laid out like the digital number eight without the lid. It was a fully catered, parentally funded bordello—*The Rear Window* meets *Animal House*, a gossip surveillance state. Only by playing the angles just right, and knowing which windows corresponded to which interest, could you get away with anything. But you had to walk proud. Slinking and shuffling were conspicuous. All the little intrigues that daily swarmed the place, and pretending they didn't affect you, was hard work. Our moral code was total disclosure. To this end there was the online registry of hookups called the Spit Web. Anyone could add to it. It was a graphic representation of all the intra-college hookups complete with our fresher photos. The three of us were together in a sparse corner with many lines linking Horace back to the main field.

One night I was woken by the sound of chairs and tables from the block's anteroom being thrown against my door. The bolt held, but in the morning my way was blocked by a mountain of furniture. I never found out who did it and never told the administration.

Her friends certainly knew that I wasn't sleeping with her. At college the judgments of groups of women often destroyed a man's chances, and they treated me very well. Every night we spent together she tried to guide me there, but I rolled away or removed her hand. She gave small harrumphs of protest but did not leave, as I feared she might. After hours of nearly silent tussle, I got up and relieved myself in the toilets. It became a private joke: what a reversal! I could see that it confused her, but what could I do? It became routine; her request, my refusal. On a hot night in October, I lost my resolve. There's nothing that can't be spoken of so why not say it? The window was open and just then a possum came through it and knocked several binders off her desk. I watched with astonishment as it dipped a claw in a half-eaten packet of Burger Rings I had brought. It looked just like a little person snacking, engrossed in the show. She shooed it back to the lemon tree outside and slammed the window.

I don't know why I didn't sleep with McCaffrey straight away. Maybe it was because I was a virgin, just come from a painfully tender yet unconsummated teenage friendship with a hometown girl. I was afraid of admitting it and of embarrassing myself in the act. I didn't know how to ask the questions you're meant to ask. "How do you know you won't get pregnant?", "Should I use a condom?" and all the rest. Could that have been the whole reason? At any rate, the night before I went back to California for the Christmas break I realized it might be my last chance. I didn't refuse her, and it seemed the easiest thing.

The emails and phone calls became fewer and fewer as the Northern winter stretched on. When I came back she was with

Horace again. On the fifth stop at the College back-to-uni pub crawl on a forty-degree day, I saw them kissing. I guess she felt that music, though mathematical, transcended science better than words.

She really did love him; it would have been so easy for her to tell me. I totally ignored her from that day on. No niceties, no acknowledgements. My vehemence surprised me. I had cared far more all along. When I sat with her and her friends at lunch, I spoke to everyone but her. If we passed each other under the ridged steel eaves late at night, I kept my head up. If she came into the computer room while I was writing an essay, I wrote all the faster. If I finished my task and she remained, I went next door to the piano room and pounded out twelve-bar blues, "The Card Cheat" and "What a Wonderful World," mouthing the words as I went.

I blamed her; with Horace I was lenient. The 3 a.m. discussions resumed and he apologised for taking her back. "You had her first," I said. Strictly speaking, I never spoke to her again.

It was Wittgenstein who said that superficial curiosity about the latest discoveries of science was "one of the lowest desires of modern people." But who wouldn't be curious about the discovery that made the colonisation of Mars possible? When I gave up literature (without giving up on it) and took the job at *Scientific Australian*, I entered a sea of untranscribed genius. Everyone was smarter and more energetic than me, but most couldn't formulate their thoughts into concise English. Sure, she wasn't one of them. She was a great populist, and it was great to receive her articles. She always addressed them to "Mr. Nathan Bactria" and professional relations were maintained. I sent back my edits, which she accepted unless I had misconstrued a technical term, in which case my error was explained courteously. I couldn't have said whether there was a rhinoceros in the room.

She had a way of making tough concepts easy with analogies and metaphor, ("say you're making instant coffee . . .") And she never condescended with gee-whiz, flash-bang borrowings from science fiction. She used the proper words for things. We ran three articles by her, one pre-launch, one during transit, and one after Asimov's first harvest. By that time of course, she was working in California, close to my hometown. She wrote out step-by-step how the settlers would grow their potatoes, apples, bananas, and wheat. I called the article, "How a Martian Bakes the Bread." That's what I did: render the ideas of others ridiculous.

The night before I returned home at the end of that salutary first year, the night I finally cracked, she told me: "I have this disorder where when I'm supposed to feel pleasure it usually registers as pain. Sometimes it snaps between the two without warning. My brain is broken. I've been to the sexual health clinic and everything."

"How long have you had it?"

"Since I can remember."

Still, she pushed me as usual. She didn't cry out, as I'd expected, in either pain or pleasure.

Love, no call it gratitude, call it that, I touched no ground when I woke the next day to pack my bags. I took my non-portables across the quad to storage on little wings. It was a sunny day, and the taxi was late. She was a tough girl and, I trust, a tough woman to the end. I lost touch with the boys and Horace years ago. What became of him and McCaffrey I never knew, but I often wondered about her. For years afterward every glimpse of red hair I caught made me tense my diaphragm.

It's inevitable I suppose that humans will end up on further planets someday, but will we ever leave earth, our primordial parent? When we die our bodies remain in the world of matter, but something goes. Goes where? It goes to the world that controls the world of matter. Is the fact of death not evidence enough of this? Many African tribes, even with the great strides in advancement made in that region, still believe all deaths are caused by sorcery . . . forgive the long letter and the felt metaphysics of an old man, my friend, but you deserve a full explanation for the refusal of your reasonable request. I still believe she wronged me, or I wronged her, it doesn't greatly matter which; it would be improper to give the last word on her life. As you age the angles temper and become as obtuse as the horizon. All luck in finding someone else.

    N.B.

# ACKNOWLEDGEMENTS

Grateful appreciation is due to the editors of the following journals in which some of these stories appeared, sometimes in slightly different form:

*Dappled Things*: "How Can We Know the Way"

*Gargouille*: "Your Eisenhower Dollar"

*Quadrant*: "Render Unto" & "Lynbrook"

*Verity La*: "The Olive Pit"

*Voiceworks*: "McCaffrey: By an Obituarist"

"McCaffrey: By an Obituarist" was highly commended in the 2012 *The Age* Short Story Award.

"it's flat food round the midriff and long food up the sleeve" is taken from Les Murray's poem "Employment for the Castes in Abeyance," from his book Ethnic Radio (Sydney: Angus and Robertson, 1977)

My thanks to Janille Stephens, Mary Finnegan, and Joshua Hren of Wiseblood Books for their extreme and irrational dedication to literature, and to George Thomas, fiction editor of *Quadrant*.

A number of these stories were completed in June 2023 during my time as artist-in-residence at Police Point Shire Park, Portsea, Victoria. My thanks to the Mornington Peninsula Shire Council and Rebecca Owens. Several stories were also completed and all of them were enhanced under the pedagogical and editorial brilliance of Katy Carl while I was the Wiseblood Books Writer-in-Residence in July

2024. I would also like to thank Matthew Gardiner, John Morrissey, Scott Arthurson, Alex Lewis, and Clarence Caddell, who read early versions of some of these stories and made helpful suggestions.

# ABOUT THE AUTHOR

Lucas Smith was born in Los Angeles to an Australian mother and American father. His fiction, poetry, and nonfiction have appeared in numerous journals, both in Australia and overseas, including *Australian Book Review, Dappled Things, Quadrant, Meanjin, Island, The Rialto,* and *The Catholic Weekly*. His fiction has been highly commended in *The Age* Short Story Award and the John Marsden Award for Young Writers. He was the June 2023 artist-in-residence at Police Point Shire Park, Portsea, Victoria, and the 2024 Wiseblood Books Writer-in-Residence. In 2020, he co-founded Bonfire Books, an independent publishing house. He lives with his wife and two daughters in Gippsland, near the southernmost edge of the Australian mainland. *Spare Us Yet* is his first book.